Witho

Bode Sowande

Longman

**Longman Group Limited
Longman House,
Burnt Mill, Harlow, Essex, UK**

Longman Nigeria Ltd
Ikeja, Ibadan, Owerri,
Zaria and representatives
throughout Nigeria

© Bode Sowande 1982

First published 1982

ISBN 0 582 78573 1

Printed in Great Britain by
Richard Clay (The Chaucer Press) Ltd,
Bungay, Suffolk

Dedicated to the affectionate
memory of my aunt, the original Mama,
Olusola Sowunmi

One

It was part of the daily routine for Bafemi to visit either the Bakery or Iya Eleko, and this was why, on a hot and still afternoon, he was trudging his way through the bush-path. Two pairs of feet parted the grass that hung over the path. Their sandals were characteristically dusty. One of the boys began to whistle as he walked on in front of the other.

'Deji, stop whistling in the sun.'

'What would that do to you, wake up your dead grandfather?' Deji's whistling rose two octaves higher.

Bafemi, the younger of the two boys, grumbled under his breath. Deji's whistling appeared to rise and fall with piercing pitch in this still afternoon. The two boys were now going past the church cemetery. Purposely, Bafemi turned his eyes away from the tombstones. Purposely, Deji stared at them.

'Any time I pass a cemetery, I want to read the inscriptions on the gravestones. Any time I open the newspaper, I don't read the news, I read the obituaries,' Deji said.

'Your mind is profane. Respect the dead. Let them rest. That's what Mama tells us.'

'That same Mama also says that heaven is a place of perfect workmanship and mastership. How can those who are working also be resting?' Deji paused at the exit of the cemetery.

'Do not disturb their work then. Mama says we should not ask too many questions, that we should begin by receiving answers ... No ... Mama says, ask questions like children because children don't know, but do not ask questions like those who assume they know ... Like you, Deji.'

The following ten minutes passed in trivial arguments over what the Sunday School taught as the divinity of

God, the workmanship of men and the child-innocence of the soul at the portal of heaven. Bafemi's voice rose. Deji's voice rose higher. Each accused the other of sin.

The church building was lost to the brow of the boulder as they climbed Kudeti hill. The small huts appeared. The mud walls of the compounds rose.

The two children did not stop arguing. They drifted from the original point to other, irrelevant topics. Neither would yield to the other. The voices of some other people rose in the distance. The scorching heat of the afternoon then existed side by side with noise. At the sound of a more voluminous rumble of other human voices, the argument of the two boys ceased. They were now about ten yards from a mud house within a large compound of other houses. They strode over the dwarf wall of the compound.

The human voices competed for dominance. For a stranger, the din would be most disturbing to a much-needed equilibrium on such a hot day. However, this was the normal sign of activity at Iya Eleko's, and it had been like this since she began her trade of *eko*, many years ago. An old man spread himself on a skeletal armchair, dozing under the shade of a tree. The old man was untouched by the noise. What permeated his being was the somnolence of such a hot day. Deji and Bafemi were indifferent to the noise. It was the sign of good trade. Noise was part of the human activity of this place. Without the din, Iya Eleko's place would be lifeless.

Goats and naked children scurried about the place. With practice, Deji and Bafemi pushed their way through as they moved into the noise. The noise took them and absorbed them. They became part of the noise. Elbows edged through the bodies. Sweat poured down the faces, but the boys burrowed their way through and with practice they arrived at the inner circle of the huge eko-room. This was the nucleus of the energy in the haggling and buying. There was a neat pattern of huge pots, rising from the ground, over the fireplaces. No one ventured beyond the pots.

In these pots white *ogi* was being boiled, after a cyclic

process that began with fermented corn. In large baskets, neatly wrapped loaves of eko were packed. Deji and Bafemi moved with ease to the baskets, which were grouped in sizes. The medium-size was the one they wanted. Iya Eleko's daughter moved nearer to them and pointed to their basket.

'I reserved this for you. That should last your household for two days. Sometimes I wonder if Mama does not over-feed you.'

Seri and Bafemi pulled the basket and in three smooth movements the basket was lifted to Bafemi's head.

Iya Eleko was sweating, glowing like ebony. She was a fleshy woman with a throaty laugh that hovered over a snarl. In her boisterous trade the laughter and the snarl had their respective purposes. She accepted the money from Deji and ran the coins down her waist ruffs of *tobi*. In a flash she was back to work.

Seri took Bafemi and Deji to the exit which was relatively calm as it opened into the rear of the compound. Along the passage young girls wrapped steaming hot eko with trained hands. Seri threw a greeting or two. The girls called back in greeting, their concentration unwavering.

The boys and Seri stepped into the back of the compound. There were more children here, running around what felt like a homely security.

'I'll see you at school tomorrow and, Deji, make sure you help Bafemi carry part of the load, even though you are older,' Seri called after them as she went back to her mother's teeming home industry.

The journey home was slower. Three times Deji relieved Bafemi of the load. The sun was sinking when they arrived home. The other children were then getting water from the tap for the evening bath. Deji went for his bath, while Bafemi went to see to his last daily duty – watering the flower beds.

In this house, on any day there never was enough time for Bafemi. There was always work to be done. Sleep – rise – prayers – work – breakfast – school – home – lunch – prayers – siesta – study – work – evening meal

– study – prayers – bed. However much he tried to squeeze time for pleasure, there was never room. Mama stood perpetually there, cane in hand. In this house there were always lessons being taught from the folktales and the Bible. He grumbled under his breath; why should there not be a single moment of rest?

As he went for his evening bath, the thought of his parents flashed through his mind. His father was in England. Within the figments of his memory he could not make out his face. Was his father a reality? The mental actuality remained in him, but the reality was not within his realisation. It was beyond him. His mother was somewhere in Abeokuta and Lagos. Somewhere, between those two towns. Again he vaguely remembered her usually tear-filled face. The hardest memory to be realised was that of Ayodele, his sister. She did not seem to exist at all.

Bafemi splashed water on his body and his senses were bathed by the soothing comfort of the water. He thoroughly enjoyed his evening bath after the day's chores. Little did he know how events were shaping for him that day. Little did he know that the sudden mind-connection he developed with his parents and sister, had to do with his mother's visit. It would seem that his feelings that evening had been aroused by a telepathic link, the gift of God. This was how Daniel, Bafemi's mentor, would explain it.

As he finished his bath, Bafemi heard his name being called by Mama. He grumbled again: 'No time to rest. I've hardly finished my bath.' He nonchalantly went about oiling his body and hair. He combed his hair at his own pace. He heard two more calls. He slowly put on his clothes. He walked slowly to the boys' room. Another call was echoed by half a dozen voices of the other children. Bafemi looked at himself in the mirror and he walked towards the call with self-directed briskness, determined to be in command these last hours of the day. He thought aloud that at least some time of the day must be free of pressure.

He ran up the stairs, turned sharply at the top and

met Deji, who said: 'It's your mother, visiting.'

Bafemi's breath came to his mouth, as he walked along the verandah that led to Mama's room. His head was now bubbling with many thoughts of a possible visit from his mother. The more he considered it, the more unlikely it seemed to him. He knocked on Mama's door with temerity and waited to be invited in. He was summoned in.

There, on an easy chair, in an angle within the large bedroom, was his mother. The flash of recognition struck his young mind. The small woman in the chair smiled. Bafemi just stood there, the door closing behind him.

'But it is your mother! Don't you know your mother again?' Mama broke the initial silence.

Truly this was his mother. The fact sank into his mind and spread all over him. Mama noiselessly walked out and closed the door behind her.

'Bafemi, it's me, your mother, Mary.'

The joy that spread and grew from within now radiated on Bafemi's face, and extended towards the mother. The room was filled with an intense feeling of love of mother for son and son for mother. Speech did not come forth. The years of separation narrowed and turned into one vibrant moment that lasted some few minutes. As the moment assumed its own character of filial affection, the son rushed at his mother, embraced her as she sat, going on his knees, overwhelmed. It was then that Mary wept silently.

Bafemi asked many questions, bent over the lap of his mother, rummaging in her bag, filled with gifts for him.

'And my sister Ayo'? Is she fine? Do you hear from my father in England? When will he be back? . . . You don't visit me often. Why? . . . '

'This is a home for you, Bafemi. Mama is your father's sister. You are home, . . . '

He looked up and saw her tears, that seemed to fill up his own eyes as well, without understanding why.

'Your father wrote from England. He wants me to go to Jos and stay with my parents. I will write to you and visit you ... even though ... Jos is more than five hundred miles away.'

Mary exercised control, but it did not prevent the room from assuming another atmosphere of loss that could only be felt by the well loving son and mother. She gathered Bafemi to herself, wiped his eyes and then gave him the gifts, very slowly.

This was when Bafemi Sotomi saw his mother last. When the memories came back, all he remembered were those two crying eyes.

Many facts remained hidden to Bafemi as Mary journeyed north to her parents. The baby girl on her lap rocked from side to side with the movement of the train. The girl, Ayodele, hardly looked at her mother's face, since the faces of the other anonymous passengers fascinated her. They were the voyage-toughened faces of the northerners; men in voluminous robes, with goatee beards that seemed to remain motionless in spite of the perpetual munching and crunching of kola-nut. There were the faces of traders from the south, tightly packed on their seats, in gangways, huddled over heavy sacks and wares. All these passengers rocked from side to side with the train. As their faces were of all types, so were their odours which contained a permanent carbon smell of coal and urine. This was a third-class coach. In between the wagons of the third class were beggars of all types, each oppressing the other, vying for room, except perhaps the lepers, furtively looking for wagon masters, who hunted them down, as outcast creatures of this human community.

It was in this train that Mary travelled home to her parents, keeping down her fear of being abandoned by a husband seeking his freedom in divorce. Up till then, her face was calm, but her mind was a raging storm of despair. It was no wonder that she attended to Ayodele, her daughter, with no particular concentration.

How could she bear the pain of the fact? Within the largeness of her heart, Mama had contemplated Mary's problem on their last meeting in Ibadan, and she promised to help. From the depth of her heart, Mama brought forth words of comfort and spread wide rippling feelings of sympathy on that last visit of Mary. It was then that Mary made the initial effort to appeal to her own mind to be strong in the face of the rushing emotions of helplessness.

The truth was that Mary in the ripeness of her early womanhood was being abandoned by Tunji her husband. The letter had come with a lucid message. He wanted a divorce and his reason was that he was in love with another woman in England.

To Mary the divorce, if it came, would – she thought – drive her mad. How could she face it? How could she start all over again? The primary thought for refuge made her decide to rehabilitate herself at her parents' home in Jos. Meanwhile Tunji's family, with the help of Mama, would try to save the situation.

Refuge first; all her feelings yearned for refuge. But first, she visited Bafemi, hiding the news from him. Next, she set out on the trip to Jos. It was an endless journey during which her eyelids succumbed to slumber and her mind ransacked the eternal corners of hopelessness. She slept and had confused dreams. Which way? she kept asking. Which way? The mind revealed labyrinths and nothing else. The more she asked for a way, the tighter was the maze of dark corridors that led nowhere. Long before the train entered Jos, the calm on Mary's face cracked and the meeting with Mama was a forlorn memory, in spite of its sympathy. Her face was no longer calm. The cry in her echoed through eternities of the mind and the face bore such intense need that could only be behind one harrowing cry of 'Help me! Help me!' At this time, Mary was merely moving among other people. She was almost drowned in the roaring storm of despair that raged in her mind.

Mary sank into her mother's arms as soon as she opened the door. She and Ayodele were now home in Jos and there was no better way of stating the reason for their coming than with the outburst of tears. Mary outpoured herself, heaving so much that within seconds her little daughter joined in.

Mary's mother shut the door on the street.

'What is the matter? What exactly is the matter? What has happened? I have been asking you ever since you came in . . . ' Then the older woman snapped; 'Will you stop crying!' By now the crumpled letter was opened for the older woman to read.

Then Mary's father came and walked his daughter to his sitting-room. It was his appearance that restored order. Mary sat on a chair. Her father looked at her and expressed his feelings.

'I don't know what it is, daughter, but before you tell me, I offer my sympathies. I also begin to wonder why our in-laws allowed you to travel unaccompanied if you brought such bad news.'

He lit his pipe. He was calm. His control affected Mary. Her storm ebbed. Her mother came in, gave the letter to her husband, folded her arms across her chest, suddenly at war with the world in her mumbled comments, all inaudible.

The man folded the letter back, and rose to his feet.

'Mary, go and wash your daughter. You need to be refreshed too. Your mother will prepare a meal for you. I was going to see a friend before you came, and now I'll go.'

'Will you do nothing about it?' the older woman yelled.

'We shall and God will. Let's have some peace in the house. Mary, it's nothing but a shadow. Tonight when the house sleeps, we'll talk about it and find a way back to some clarity.'

With that he went out. Neither of the women saw the shadow across his face. It appeared only in an instant and disappeared only in an instant. As he went on his lonely walk, he muttered prayers under his breath. 'This is a real problem,' he said in his mind, 'but we'll fight back, and we'll win.'

Mary's calm was restored by her father's attitude. Suddenly she felt as if what had happened was not true, as if it had never existed. She began to settle down at home. Her mother was troubled, and she did not hide

8

her feelings. Even, she hoped that Mary's father would hurry back with the 'miracle solution' that glowed on his face just before he went out.

His return brought no such 'miracle solution' as the two women were to learn later that evening. The house was peaceful when he told them quietly:

'I do not know of any solution except to appeal to his senses. I know that it is the bug that bites our sons when they go abroad. They are separated from loved ones. They are lonely. They meet sympathisers and they become infatuated ... That is a category. Some are genuinely in love. But Tunji ... '

He remained silent. The women did not speak. Then he continued: 'Your mother and I share your pain with you, Mary, and we shall live to share your comfort when things return to normal. But first tell me what you have done or plan to do.'

By then Mary was remarkably calm. Like all normal people, Mary had three parts in her. A part belonged to her father, the second part belonged to her mother, while the third part was the way she evolved her own character. Her father was an unusually calm and strong character, the type who could bear tides and ebbs like ... perhaps some ancient fathers or saints. Her mother was always in flusters when the wind raised the slightest dust of opposition. Her mother could dance and sing when Providence gave her joy. Mary used more of her father's temperament whenever her mother's was quickly brought under control. And so she said to her parents in that evening shadow:

'I have not done anything significant yet. I have not written to Tunji. I visited Bafemi and lied to him that his father asked me to come here. I told Mama, Tunji's sister, and she has promised to write. Mama said I should pray.'

Mary stopped and looked into her palms for a long time. She raised her head. Her father noticed the strong glint in her eyes. Her mother twitched nervously.

Mary continued: 'And I believe in prayers ... very strongly. I believe that Tunji will come back to me. I love him. I love him very much. I have known no other man in my life except him and I will know no other. I will wait for him.'

'Suppose he does not come back like so many of these men when they go abroad? Or suppose if he comes back home he does not want you any more?' Her mother's voice had a depth of anxiety in it.

'Mother, he *will* come back.' Mary said.

Her father added in a flat voice: 'Some men don't come back. Suppose he doesn't, will you marry again ... let us say in three years to come?'

'He will come back, father,' she said again. No one said anything for a long time. The night was filled with silence. Mary's voice floated again. 'He will come back, even if it is to be in eternity.'

Her mother grunted. Her father got to his feet. The talk was over. Mary announced finally that she would write to Tunji. They went to bed.

The following months were spent on overland and transatlantic correspondence. Tunji did not reply to a single letter. Mary fasted. She begged God. She begged the saints. She lost flesh, and some freshness. The months threatened to become years. Her father would appeal to her to re-marry. Her mother would make many trips to the south, to Tunji's relatives. Nothing worked. Tunji only sent money to Mama for Bafemi's keep.

Bafemi was growing, not under the wing of his parents, but of an aunt. Even then, the boy knew vaguely that a vital thing was lacking in his existence. It was very difficult for him to express it for he was nothing but a child at that time.

Two

Wednesdays were for art and craft at Bayo Cole's studio. Bayo Cole was Bafemi's cousin and his private art teacher. Other than going to the art and craft studio, Bafemi spent a few minutes on Wednesday, visiting his mentor, Daniel. It was also his best day for saving money. He sometimes decided to walk the dusty road on his outward and homeward journey, adding up a trek of four miles, and increasing his savings by fifty kobo. This saving came from the unspent taxi-fares.

Bafemi pattered along the dusty road to Molete, after crossing the age-old Kudeti River, a ravaging part of the Ogunpa River. The only comfortable part of the trek was the passage through the banana grove. At least, it was comfortable when the rains were receding to the sea and Kudeti River looked gentle and less mucky. On those days Bafemi carved as many grooves as possible on the crepe of the banana tree, watching the sap flow to the ground, on which some alligators crawled harmlessly. He would finally leave the enveloping coolness of this small grove, walk through the beds of a vegetable farm, and climb back to the road. Then he felt the heat of the sun in the dry sand. It made him walk briskly.

Bafemi arrived at the studio on time. There never was any question of lateness since Mama always made sure he set out early, giving him enough time for the art sessions.

Bayo Cole was sweating among chopped trunks of wood in the backyard of his studio. He looked up casually at Bafemi.

'All right with you, my little apprentice?'

'Yes, cousin Bayo. I saw some more alligators today.'

'You must be very careful among those reptiles. Some of them are dangerous.'

'They are harmless, cousin Bayo. At least these ones are. They seem to know when I arrive. I watch them feed on the insects. It's best watching them slide into the water, and swim across.'

'Aren't you afraid of them? They have forked tongues that suck your brains out through the nostrils ... ' Bayo was laughing menacingly.

'They don't do that to the vegetable farm boys. They are harmless. And God will prevent them from harming me.'

'They won't harm you. I was only joking. Those ones are mere overgrown lizards. Well, shall we carve an alligator then?'

Bayo tossed a square board at Bafemi. 'We'll continue from our last craft lesson. Board-carving. And the subject is *An alligator on the ground*. Simple. Let's get started.'

Teacher and boy went into the small studio. Bafemi picked his favourite nook and settled down. First he made a thick pencil impression of what he thought an alligator looked like. Then he began to etch round the outline with a lightweight chisel. His afternoon lesson began.

Bayo watched him and marvelled. To him Bafemi was simply Mama's boy. Lately this was what others also called him. 'Mama's son' or 'Mama's boy' and it was obvious that Mama was shaping his character as best she could. The first year of grooming was over when Bafemi became six. He was already big for his age. He had been sent to school by Mama a year earlier than the required school age of six and proved to be an encouraging pupil. Bayo remembered that Mary's last visit to her son was at the beginning of his first year at school, and it was clear to Bayo that Bafemi had known his mother only vaguely for two years, within a child's consciousness. Between the ages of two and four he knew her as children of his age do know their mothers. Between four and five he was brought to Mama, and Bafemi readily took affectionately to Mama as both mother and father.

'Occupy a child's mind productively, guide it religiously and you will shape his character': this was

Mama's view. It was also her hope; an only hope to blot out of the mind of this child any impression of separation from his father and mother. Mama worked hard at his grooming. Indeed it was no less noble than the grooming given to children at a royal court. In all its glory this grooming bordered on elitism. This was Bayo's conclusion.

'Nevertheless, I like him, my boy apprentice. Perhaps if I could guide him for the next few years, perhaps six, he would or could become a master of his art. Maybe.'

The advantage that Bafemi had at this stage of his life was that unlike some children of broken marriages, he was not abandoned. On the other hand, he was surrounded by an aunt, a cousin and a mentor, all ambitiously keen to help him. If he did not know this sharply now, his mind was set to examine it critically later on. If these God-sent helpers succeeded with their ambitious plans for him, Bafemi would become a grown-up of sterling character. As all the factors of probability prove, the truth of the realisations might fall short, very short of these designs.

This was the way Daniel saw it, and this agreed solely with his faith in prayers. The best would happen with prayers.

'Did you call on the Adept on your way here, Bafemi?'

'Who?'

'Daniel, whom you refer to as Woli,'

'No, but I will call on him on my way home.' Bafemi eased up his position. 'Cousin Bayo, what is an Adept?'

'Mmm. A man who knows a lot and still learns a lot in order to know more, and practises the value of what he knows. That is an Adept. Let us leave it at that for now. You will understand it fully later on.'

'Is every Adept a Woli?'

'Woli means the prophet and I presume before a man has the gift of fore-knowledge, he must be a constant companion of knowledge. And so Woli may belong to a special class of Adepts. As I said, you will understand this later on. Shall we say that we need to be in Primary

One before we can progress to other places of learning?'

'And someone becomes an Adept?'

'Yes ... why not, if one is always knowing and seeking. You may as well want to drain the water of a fountain ... The hair turns grey and one is still learning how to be an Adept. You understand?'

'Yes ... Granny for instance knows more than Mama and us, but she is still learning.'

'Very good. And the Adept would say, it goes on for ever and ever.'

'Even when we die?'

'Even when we die. You ask him tonight. Now continue working on your own, and at closing time meet me at the Adept's. You should finish that carving before next Wednesday. Then you'll sandpaper it. And we go into another step of our practice. And as they tell you at school ... Practice ... '

'Practice makes perfect.'

'Very well. Meet me at closing time.' Bayo Cole left Bafemi working in the studio, with trust. The boy apprentice continued to work, his mind growing with the work and the work growing with his mind.

Would it be too ambitious, Bayo asked himself, to see Bafemi as the child apprentice in the studio and the acolyte or neophyte at the Adept's? If apprenticeship was the experience and learning of the processes and steps towards perfection, it stood to reason that this child apprentice might also have the gift of the Grace to become an acolyte, for according to the Adept, one needed to be awakened to the Grace that was always giving. Perhaps Bafemi would be awakened.

It all seemed very ambitious, but this was the way Bayo always considered Bafemi's progress.

'As for me, I am already totally without discipline, except in my art. I regard myself as being vulgar, but the child apprentice should be guided until he makes up his mind. To receive the Grace of the Great Flux or get bogged down by all the vulgarity, which gave birth to him in the first place.' Bayo saw the anonymous alleyway that led to the largeness of the Adept's.

He walked on and reached the sandy opening, the mouth of the large expanse in which the Adept had his work done. Mud buildings stood as if unattached in a careful triangular formation. These mud houses numbered seven. Beyond them was the wall that hid the garden from view. It was an air garden that led to a part of the flowing Kudeti River. This garden had never experienced any flood in all the ravaging history and tradition of the river. Many years before, the Adept received the plot of land as a gift from a council of chiefs in the city. There, he was to carry on his work.

Bayo entered the Adept's central oval, the mud structure nearest to the garden wall. A water lamp glowed where the Adept was bent over some books, peacefully reading. Bayo still marvelled at that lamp, a gift from a foreign visitor.

The Adept looked up and smiled:

'And how is the intellectual? Still convinced that the vulgar mind needs no Grace, if the hands can mould the perfection to glorify the Flux?'

'Yes. This artist is without redemption.'

'No matter what effort he makes?'

'Regardless of his efforts.'

'Well then, perhaps we should ask after the child apprentice. How goes his work?'

'Satisfactory. He will call on you tonight, on his way home.'

'Alas, I may be at work.' He rose to his full height. 'We have made a major victory. I cannot stop at thanking the Cosmic. The leprous skin healed up, the bones re-formed, the blood was purified, and a new man is born in the good image of the Soul, all broken laws atoned for.'

His voice was joyful, but his face told more of the story. Its self-illumination reached out in radiance.

'Many others will be brought, to set aright the laws that were broken. As I say, Bayo, no man should be ill, except when the rules and rhythms are broken. Give man back the rhythm and he will be well. We pray day and night for that.'

'I do not know how to give you my compliments, Woli.'

'Me, compliments? You must be joking. Me? Direct your compliments to the Cosmic and the beyond, without saying anything to man.'

'Any mass-media coverage?' Bayo mused.

'You meant that as a joke, I hope.'

The events and happenings at the Adept's received no news coverage. They had no signboard to advertise themselves, nor did they receive any pay for the work done. This was a place completely shut to the world, yet existing actively within it. The secrecy was self-imposed and those who gained from this place of rehabilitation of the mind and body observed the silent norm of worship. Many had been rehabilitated, but their vow and promise before healing was to *tell no one*, except the God of their Hearts. The Adept believed this was the gateway to worship and that the rehabilitation of the mind and the body was worship not of man but of God. Why then, the statement went, should man advertise his worship of God by the words of his mouth?

Those who received the rehabilitation of the mind and body at the Adept's could only be known by perhaps their change of attitude and their strict obedience of the axiom: '*Iwa lẹ sin, Iwa rere, ju ogun lo*: True evangelism is through the behaviour and good behaviour guarantees Peace Profound.'

The Adept said the Peace that was Profound could only be found in the perfect mind and body, and the work for perfection was infinite.

All this was unknown to Bafemi but made known to Bayo.

'Bayo, you will worship,' the Adept said. 'The sign is there, the awareness is there. Now it is obvious that you revolt against it.'

'You mean Bell and Bible in the streets?' Bayo covered his face with his hands in disgust. 'No.'

'We shall not argue, for you will make your own choice. Meanwhile I must go. Why not spend some moments in the back garden? It is well lit with a hundred oil lamps. The atmosphere will help your thoughts. Or do you prefer to watch the bone-setters or the herb-mixers? They know you, their intellectual.'

With that Daniel disappeared into the large compound.

Bayo remained in the room, temporarily raging within himself. 'I'll tell him not to call me the intellectual! It seems an empty word these days.' He went out, into the garden.

If the rehabilitated did not tell, how then did people keep coming? Bayo wondered for a while and remembered what the Adept called the pull of attraction for those who believed. That was it. This strange phenomenon of 'pull' or magnetism of the faithful guaranteed the constant attendance of the 'faithful'.

Was this man a magician? A fake, another Rasputin? Bayo roamed the garden aimlessly; but why should he always doubt this man? Why? Why should he always resist his inner urge for this knowledge? Why did he refuse to bend his knees, to worship, but prefer to see what wonders the Grace would perform first in the child-apprentice?

Bayo heard what sounded like a soft human voice. Curiously and cautiously he changed his direction and walked towards the voice. Then he stopped. The man who was talking was naked, his head clean-shaven. Had he just come out of the water and wandered into the garden? It seemed strange to Bayo that at that early part of the evening a man would strip himself completely and bathe, in what could be a partially open view. He remembered the wood-cutters from a northern tribe. They bathed in broad daylight, naked, under Kudeti bridge.

The naked man in the garden squatted and resigned himself easily to that position. Then he began to sing, aloud. His voice rang into the gathering night, lacking the melody of an evensong. Bayo trembled, in spite of himself. He tip-toed backwards as noiselessly as he could. Within a safe distance, he watched the naked man.

'It's disgusting! Disgusting!' Bayo hissed under his breath.

'Yes it is, it's man's handiwork.' Bayo's eyes popped out of his head in fear. He swung round, gasping. It was the Adept looking towards the naked man. The force that Bayo felt went through every part of his veins, running down the fountain track of his spinal column. He thought it was the 'fear'. Then he felt a sudden clarity of mind, joyful in its lucidity and he looked strangely at the Adept.

The Adept did not consider Bayo any more. He was not at that moment looking or talking to him. The artist's inner being caught the vibrations, outpouring from this huge man, overpowering in its goodness. Within the concentration of Daniel, the singing naked man rose to his feet, his song dying out. The song did not ebb out because life went out of it, yet it died because it was cut away from its senselessness. The naked man turned in his nudity and saw Daniel. Every sensory faculty in Bayo was opening with remarkable clarity, feeling out in strength in the intangible ethers of their experience. His eyes were seeing more, his ears hearing more, his nose smelling more, his mouth tasting more and his body feeling more – feeling more and asking nothing for an explanation.

Two sparsely covered men came into the garden, carrying some clothes that Bayo presumed belonged to the naked man.

'Iretade, why did you have to undress before going out?' the first man asked.

'Don't you know that you have nothing on?' the second man said.

Iretade looked over himself and the bush, his shame could be slightly felt. He took the clothes, calmly put them on and followed the men back to the house.

The Adept took in a deep breath of air and walked towards the water edge. Bayo gradually felt the elation of the past few moments slip away from him. He looked around him and from inside him came the awe that followed the happening of any natural law which vulgar minds referred to as miracles. He looked strangely at Daniel and announced:

'I am going to get drunk tonight, Woli. I am going to get so drunk that I will forget what I have seen or felt.'

Daniel watched Bayo curiously. 'What have you felt?'

'An overpowering sense of miracle.'

'There are no such things as miracles, only divine, natural laws.'

'Was he not mad? That naked man was one of those in your clinic, was he not?'

'We run no clinic. People are rehabilitated here, among men and women who help as auxiliaries. That man was mad and brought in yesterday. He has been bathed, shaved and given clean clothes. He lives among those who help him in his rehabilitation. We do not chain or tranquillise our friends. Unfortunately, when they are here the first two or three days, we have to prepare ourselves for eventualities, such as you have seen.'

'It is dangerous. They could prey on their friends.'

'No. As you want to know, I will tell you the basic rule of our care. We believe that there is only one root to illness and only one cure. The root is the lack of balance between the attractions, repulsions, cohesions, of the related elements. The cure is a restoration of the balance. The Grace gives forth the energy of restoration. When those who need help come, they are aided by the fact that the Grace is intensely present here, because our work is to receive it constantly. Let me tell you that our occupation is not very easy. We work, always. However, it is very pleasing. The Master himself worked with the Twelve non-stop and he is still working.'

'There is more to it than that. You hypnotised that man!' Bayo protested.

The Adept felt the edge of attack in Bayo's statement. He looked away and cast his eyes into the distance. His voice, when it came, was from that distance, the kind that held one's attention by its will.

'I did not hypnotise him. I tell you this because I see

that you are very curious to seek and know. You do not learn by discrediting first and eliminating other hypotheses. That is vulgar science. The higher sciences and the Arts deal with the perfect laws.

'I did not hypnotise him, I merely helped re-open the link that he has with the Grace. It is a physical feat with a guidance of the Divine. We do not play with the plastic pleasure of magic, Bayo, we are scientists and artists, not the vulgar scientists, and not the vulgar artists. We prefer the upper part of the scale and it is hard work, like the path to the Grace.'

With that the Adept turned and went away, apparently back to work. Bayo felt uneasy. He realised that most of the moments he spent with Daniel were spent in debate, and while the Adept always remained calm, he felt too doubtful to accept that he knew nothing. It was not wrong to doubt; this he believed. However, the Adept once said that doubt sprouted from fear which was also a lack of faith. Bayo repeated to himself that it was perfectly normal to doubt.

He lit a cigarette and wondered what the face of Thomas had looked like when he first heard of the Resurrection.

'I must get drunk tonight. Get drunk and, if I can, sleep with a woman. Later I may paint Thomas. First, I'll get drunk.'

As he made his way out of the Adept's, he met Bafemi.

'Oh, are you leaving, Cousin Bayo?' The boy's eyes were so innocent that for a moment Bayo envied his child-world.

'I'll wait here for you. Go and say good evening to the Adept. You have five minutes. I have a feeling he may be busy. You know where to ask.'

Bafemi ran into the Adept's mud house. Bayo smoked on. He said to himself: 'I must stop being nervous.' He convinced himself that he needed time; as much time as possible to relate himself to what Daniel referred to as the Grace. Meanwhile his mind was re-focused on his imminent pub-crawl.

The streets that ran on the outside of the area already

teemed with people, hurrying home or strolling out. The horns of taxis reached Bayo from the streets. He looked up at the sky mechanically. The sky held a profundity at this time of the night. It was clear and promised no rain. He looked round him as people milled past the mud houses, seemingly unaware of this nucleus of tremendous activity. They walked along the wall that led to the garden and turned on their homeward paths. The anonymity of the Adept gave Bayo more amazing feeling when he watched the people walk past. Not a curious glance was cast by anyone on hearing any sound or seeing any strange thing. The place gave no strange revelations to the curious nor did it afford any amusement to the idle as perhaps the building of a prison might or the decay of the Government Hospital would. No extraordinary sensation could be experienced by walking around these mud houses and the outer wall of the garden. Bayo Cole critically observed each passer-by. They were all the usual subjects of the crowds, the idle pedestrians.

But what happened to the few who entered? What did they feel? The artist inhaled his cigarette and imagined the rush of oppressed housewives seeking consolation in the church, or the lonely, continuously drawn to the company of his lifeless beer bottle in the pub, or the young men dashing to the dance hall. The same pull took a certain degree of will from the individual that went to fulfil his desire. Was the individual merely escaping, or was he fully enjoying living, consuming these moments of his pleasures? How was one to know that he received the Grace because of fear of being punished, hereafter or for the creative pleasure of it? As long as the fear was present, Bayo felt, he did not need to touch this Grace. The fear of what would happen afterwards must be eliminated first. The Grace would touch him, not because he feared, but because he wanted it, and he would want to live, and love it. At that moment, he did not have that desire, and that was it!

Bafemi came out, bubbling with joy, waving a piece

of paper in hand. Bayo looked at it. On it was written the Lord's Prayer. In there with the Adept, the child apprentice made the promise to learn with the Adept the use of the Lord's Prayer.

'It is simple, my son, but our lessons and their application will be on every Wednesday for one hour after the art lessons. I'll see Bayo about it. Don't tell him yet.'

Bafemi said nothing but wondered at what the Lord's Prayer needed to offer him after he had already learnt how to recite it forwards, backwards and perhaps sideways. Bayo called a taxi and he took Bafemi home to Mama. Another Wednesday ended for the child apprentice.

The older artist went again into the streets, seeking to pacify himself with beer from the pub and wishing to have a woman for the night. He entered into the night and the night took him, gave him her pleasures, her indulgence, and left him at dawn with his whole being hung-over. His body was shamelessly spent on beer and a casually known woman.

Three

The cablegram simply read: MOTHER IS ILL CONTACT HER. BAFEMI. Tunji Sotomi, the recipient of the urgent news, read through the cablegram again for the umpteenth time.

Here in England when he took his decision to ask for a divorce he was prepared for the rush of the letters that would follow. He had premeditated his decision, and anticipated the reaction of Mary and of other relatives. He knew that the pressures of the people would be brought to bear on him. The letters that his decision attracted were constantly burnt, as they arrived. A word was enough to discern the content of the letter. Sometimes it was a phrase and he met the shock reactions squarely because he was determined not to change his mind. He was not even prepared to ask himself why; not at that stage.

Gradually the letters ran into trickles and finally stopped. When this happened he was beginning to live under the conviction that he was not suited for marriage. A life of celibacy would give him independence and air-free liberty. The demand for a divorce came as a measure to apply a halt while the two parties were still young. A sound education insurance policy was drawn up for the children, Bafemi and Ayodele, and their father Tunji Sotomi began to relax and live as he thought a celibate should.

It comforted him to come home, in London, to his flat, and be fed, and danced to by Kate or Jasmine or even Fay; all at the expense of the international scholarship programme he used for his special studies on architecture. It delighted him when a new tie arrived through the post from a widow who proclaimed a tremendous admiration for his rich taste for wine, food, clothes and music. This young man in his early thirties indeed had certain pleasures that could be classified as epicurean. In his brilliance, with his opportunities and his physical strength and beauty there appeared a recklessness that might have been tamed, had it surfaced early in his life. The surprise at home sprang from this ignorance of the potential abuse of his moral and physical beauty.

Tunji Sotomi was just rejoicing at being 'left alone' when the cable came in. He ran a quick bath and shouted from the bathroom.

'Fay, my toast as usual!' A hum from last night's 'jig' escaped his breath. He ran his mind over his accounts. A few cheques came in from the B.B.C. for his participation in the regular external broadcast. His grant should have been paid into his account.

Out of the bath, and dried, he made for his room and picked up the phone.

'Give me International please ... Please I'd like to book a call to Nigeria.' He gave Mama's number in Ibadan. 'I'll receive it tonight from 8.oo ... Thank you.' He hung up.

'Is anything wrong 'Toon-jie?'

'No, Fay. I got a cable from my son.' She read it and put it back on the side table.

'Will you have to go home?'

'No, Fay, not until I know what is the matter. If it is very serious, I may have to go as a formality ... Why is your face dropping? I have told them that I'll have nothing more to do with marriage and it is final.'

She climbed back into bed, smoking. She watched him dress. 'I'll be working from two till seven today,' she said. He answered under his breath, and went for his breakfast. Last night's tape came to life from his multi-stereo set. The music had an early morning life in its wildness. Tunji took his diary, and went through his programme for the day. It included a lunch date with the middle-aged widow. He popped his head round the bedroom door.

'I'll be back by seven.' His footsteps banged down the stairs. The rev of his car reached Fay in the bedroom. In her mind's eye, she imagined him leaving.

The Rover 2000 slipped into the seven o'clock London traffic. Tunji's mind went back to his 'ex-wife', Mary. He whispered: 'Why will she not let me be? She is young. Let her remarry. Why fall sick? Could she not start living again?'

In the room, Fay, the English girl, closed her eyes, thinking how strongly she was attached to him. She was not made for analytical self-examination. 'I love him.' This was all she knew, apart from the fact that the girls in his life, including the older women, could as well be given ciphers as labels. They did not go into him to know him. They were nothing but the 'birds' who flew in and out of his nest as they pleased, and as he wanted them. There never had been the bother to evolve a female character around him and call her his woman. His non-commitment was evident, except in its physical dimensions.

'Easy come – easy go.' Fay turned on her side waiting for eight to strike. As for her, the thought of being maritally joined to any man never crossed her mind. She always explored that possibility of knowing a man, feeling for him in her own way without the obligation of marriage. She grew up at a time when the divorce rate was astronomical and she preferred to keep away from the type of emotional injury which followed broken marriages. She never would decide to give it a trial. Never!

At eight, Fay got out of bed and began to tidy up the flat. The stereo boomed across the apartment until past noon, when she went to the bus stop. She knew that she was just another girl in Tunji's life. He knew nothing about her, and he never bothered to know. Perhaps in two days she would go back to her bedsit until they had another date. He had a way of bringing his girl friends home after a date. And they had a habit of leaving for work from his place, returning with a few changing clothes and spending a few extra days.

Mary made her way into the church. It was night and

the interior of the church was lit. One Bible class was going on in the vast building. She chose a corner at the back and knelt down.

She had been doing this for several months which she did not bother to divide into years. Prayer had been her only support and lately it had become a gossamer film of protection round her. It was a protection she cherished and lived in. Soon she became so jealous of it that she guarded it from others, and kept it to herself, shutting herself into it until the time came when she did not realise how fast and thick the filmy layer was cutting her off from the world. This protection was the act she called prayers, the indulgence she called contemplation, the practice she called imagination and the hope she sought in meditation. Alas, Mary could not transcend the layer. It was as thin as ether, as strong as vibration and as intangible as air. She was now more than an introvert. Her mind, previously unsuspecting, unprepared and untrained, obliged her to its ultimate limits.

Her mind yielded to the prayers and danced in hopes. It yielded to all the disciplines she suggestively commanded until it assumed the roles as habits. Mary did not need to look at the time on her watch to know the prayer time. She could close her eyes and let her mind lead her to the church. She did not need to speak and utter her prayers. Every act had that mark of routine and this routine had gradually sapped the life out of this mind she so much depended on.

In a way, it was not her fault. Her mind, like all minds, grew in faith or hope. At that time, hope refused to touch this mind until, exhausted of its own repeated self-creations, it began to slow down in its functions. And Mary did not know. She could not know.

Her mother was confused. She had spent much time travelling to the south to confer with Tunji's family. Her mother in turn turned on the father. He had admired his daughter's courage at the beginning. It reflected an aspect of one of his own virtues, but gradually he saw reason for alarm in the extreme abuse of this positive behaviour. He saw what he thought was a virtue turn into a destructive force and plainly he began to fear.

'Will you not marry again, Mary? You look remarkably fresh. Another man may make you happy. Tunji may have been the wrong type for you.'

'Tunji is my trial,' she said.

He pleaded at other times, changing his methods, joking, chiding, threatening, until she recognised them through repetitions and they became ineffectual. Then he panicked. He sent her mother to the south to Mama, to give a full report. This was to save her daughter.

It would be laughable to the people, as well as to Mary, if her father ever suggested that she was not what a normal person should be. It was because she was well dressed, harmless, courteous, and overwhelmingly pious, and extreme piety could not be termed madness, neither could serenity be an idiosyncrasy.

And so, her father watched her, eyeing her, spying on her, while he waited for her mother's return from the south. Once he read a letter that Mary left unposted to Tunji and Bafemi. They conveyed nothing but prayers, or what could be termed lengthy epistles. It only added to his fears.

Mary was not now aware of her father's emotions, nor did she bother to ask why her mother travelled south. She simply went to church.

On that night, while she knelt, and the Bible class went on, Mary could not pray. Even the mind could no more react to the automation of the routine. She rose from the blankness of ten minutes, smiled emptily and walked home. It was that smile which refused to disappear that shook her father, until he asked hoarsely:

'Are you all right, Mary?'

And she answered: 'May God bless you, father, and mother and my children. May God forgive Tunji, for he knows not what he does.'

Her father said nothing. He observed her keenly until she went to bed. He went out into the night, heading for the Telephone Exchange, where he had a friend. He made a very long phone call to Mama.

The next day, Mama sent the cable to London. Mary's father took his little grand-daughter Ayo and put her in his sister's care. The next evening, Mary simply obeyed her father, getting into a taxi, driving into a hospital.

At the hospital gate, her face broke into a protest. She cried and protested like a child and as she was led in, all the suppressed pains of several months erupted into a thousand cries, that only a rebelling infant would make.

All her father could do was to pray. She was admitted into hospital. And he prayed, sincerely and profoundly.

Tunji was doing well in his post-graduate attachment to the London firm of builders and environmentalists; the Exe Company of Environment. He had built up a good reputation as an earnest worker, a talented designer of what the firm referred to as environment. Clearly, the firm wanted to keep Tunji, not only in England, but also in West Africa, with a base in Nigeria. Environment, the firm believed, would reinstate man in society and remove his neuroses, improve his longevity. E.C.E. occupied a four-floor part of a building, and was fully backed by a heavy investment.

As Tunji went into the research library of the firm, the librarian handed him a note. He was to report in the board room as soon as he arrived. He straightened his tie, and his pocket handkerchief. He walked briskly to the board room. There were three men inside the room; the chairman of the board, Tunji's supervisor, and the financial consultant.

'Sit down, Mr Sotomi,' the chairman said and proceeded almost immediately: 'I have read the draft of the paper that you intend to publish in the magazine *New Environment* and I like it very much. We all like it and we would like you to sell it to us.'

Tunji remained impassive. The chairman continued: 'I personally believed, Toon-jie, that pearls should not be cast before swine. Your paper contains pearls that could win men the environment of the future. We want to buy this paper.'

Tunji was thinking deeply, his mind working fast, but his face betrayed nothing. The members of the board exchanged glances a little nervously.

'You see, Tunji,' – his supervisor was the only one in England who ever pronounced his name correctly – 'the firm believes that your research has finally yielded fruit. Your plan to change Nigerian villages is ingenious and, what is more, it is inexpensive, and significantly healthy. We shall want to invest in it and open a market in Nigeria. You will, we hope, assist us. It is my strong recommendation that you should now write up your thesis, and I will be ready to call up a panel for you at the University. Hopefully, you will obtain your doctorate.'

Tunji shifted in his seat for the first time.

'My department will set up a programme on the first financial venture of the project,' the financial consultant added.

'We would like to know what you feel, Mr Sotomi?'

Tunji remained silent for a while and when he spoke he had his emotions under control.

'Gentlemen, I have only used the traditional method of the communal environment of my people. The self-regenerating cyclic process of utility supplies, like water, electricity, ventilation and so on, I have borrowed from the various experimental kibbutzim or communes in Israel and in the U.S.A. I believe very sincerely in making environment a cheap commodity. This is where I differ principally from the others. And that is how my people can benefit from it. My paper was developed around a remodelling of my people's traditional commune, an introduction of the cheap use of solar energy, the positioning of communes to the harmonious flow of air, and water, and above all the cheap use of mud for building.

'Mud houses, gentlemen, have lasted over a century at home. I believe that with the mixture of the new type of cement, we shall arrive at a longer lasting environment. However, I must insist that this project has more details which I shall only produce on the condition that it is used in Africa, cheaply and for the people. Secondly, I can only sell it at the price of a major share in the company.'

The board room was silent while it recovered from the well projected personality of Tunji Sotomi.

'Very well, Mr Sotomi, we accept the deal. You sound shrewd enough to be an entrepreneur and virtuous enough for your people. Today we shall apply to the Home Office on your behalf for a work permit. You will remain in England for two years. The project will then be launched. Meanwhile the subject will go into our top secret files. The board will be meeting in full in one hour's time. You will be called in again, your contract will be signed, and if you need any legal advice, Tom Wilson, your supervisor will give you a directory of competent mercantile lawyers.'

The brief meeting ended. Tunji went back into the elevator. It took him to the library. He was overwhelmed. He began to sweat. He took out a cigarette and smoked it. Ten minutes later, he descended into the London street and joined the urban throng.

The cablegram and now this; it was too much for one day.

Tunji got back to E.C.E. five minutes before he was due to meet the full board. The discussion re-opened and eventually closed to everyone's satisfaction.

E.C.E. was going to woo Nigeria, and benefit from her agro-industrial economy, befriending her rural people and giving hope back to the de-vitalised souls in the urban centres. Tunji was to undergo the training necessary to head such a firm and Ibadan was to be his base. The farmers, the co-operative union and the private estate agents would form the network. The plan had been drawn up with clockwork precision and Tunji was awed by the scientific minds of these men with whom he worked. He embraced fortune's gifts as they fell at his feet that day.

He got home at seven forty-five, cancelling his date

with the widow. He divulged nothing to Fay, since she mattered little to him. It came naturally to Tunji to use secrecy in all the affairs of his life. He also had the singular strength of determination which he used to guide and obey the ethics of his responsibilities at work and study.

He had a hot meal; Fay's idea of a curry with rice. Then he waited for his phone call. At nine o'clock he called the operator. There were many international calls and he had to wait for one more hour. At ten there was still no luck. He made a cup of coffee, took his brief-case and began to go through the notes of his thesis. 'Environment: the moral and physical need for man's rehabilitation in Nigeria.'

Fay was sprawled as usual on the floor, near the fireplace, listening to a pop music programme on B.B.C. He hardly noticed her as he gradually gave the subject all his attention. He noted several geographical details and underlined a question: 'What makes a community work and live?' It was in answering this question that he hoped to show the morality of environment with regard to the community.

At eleven, he closed his files, made another coffee. He was making for the phone when it rang.

'Is that Mr Sotomi? ... Mr Sotomi ... '

'Yes?'

'Hold on for your call to Nigeria ... Nigeria ... Nigeria ... is that Lagos?'

'Yes, Lagos hearing you loud and clear.' The familiar heavy accent came through, perhaps from the middle of the habitual chit chat.

'Lagos, we want Ibadan ... is that Nigeria? ... ' There was a brief wait filled with telegraphic whines and whistles.

'Ibadan.' The voice came in another brand of the accent that endeavoured to anglicise the age-old African name. London gave the number. Another pause of keyboard switches went before the line became clear.

'London. International ... '

'Yes, receiving ... Mr Sotomi, you are through.'

Mama's voice reached him. It was one of those moments of scientific triumph, when the man who cared gave thanks to the power of intelligence. Space and time were reduced to nil.

'Sister, it's me, Tunji. Can you hear me?'

'Tunji!' she exclaimed: 'Incredible. This is incredible ...' Then she remained silent as the expensive seconds ticked by into minutes.

'I saw the cable this morning.'

When she recovered from the shock, it was with an avalanche of rebuke. Her anger stung his ears.

'If you were not my own brother, born and bred a Christian, if you were a Keferi, we would say we are not surprised, but you, born and washed at birth with clear waters ... born properly but behaving like one whose soul has no call of habitation ... I counted the letters as I wrote them. You refused to reply. I refused to stop. Yet I prayed for you, prayed that the devil may not use you. Your wife wrote you, did she not? The poor girl! She begged you for what she did not know. She was well married, remember; well married, not like those useless girls who run around. What have you done with your soul? Lost it?'

She coughed and sniffed, and soon at his end he realised that she was sobbing. The minutes ticked by. He dared not hurry her. He had to endure the rising cost of the phone call. When she stopped sobbing, she began to pray and plead.

'Tunji, you whom I brought up when our parents died ... As the lost hunting mongrel heard the whistle, so will you make straight for home. The Almighty will forgive you. He will forgive you, and over there always say Amen, for I am always praying for you.' She paused and he quickly put in:

'Is she still ill?'

'Very.'

'I am sorry.'

'Is that all you can say? ... Christ have mercy.' Silence. 'Just what do you think you are, a whiteman who takes a wife today and chucks her out tomorrow?

Listen very well, if you come home with a white girl, we'll send her packing. If you come home with a black girl, we'll give ger a thrashing and if it's a brown one, we'll make her homeless . . . Oh you'll make us sin, make us sin . . . '

'Sister, please stop being emotional. Tell me exactly what is wrong.'

'You listen and you'll hear. That good girl has suffered enough, for doing absolutely nothing. It has been too long an endurance and now she is ill. The best that one could accept is a nervous breakdown . . . We only pray that it's not worse . . . ' She abused him again, stopped and began to plead, 'Write to her Tunji.'

'It's no use, sister. It's too late.'

'What do you mean, it's too late?'

'With a breakdown like that, she will recover with a better acceptance of reality. That's what the doctors do to help them. She will learn to face reality and start living again.'

'Science! Science! Christ King of Glory, have mercy! Is this all they teach you in England? Have you no humanity left?' The question pierced him through and reached his conscience for a moment. He sank into a long pause, hearing no more of what she said, and then he faintly heard her plead again.

'Please, Tunji, for the sake of your children, for the love of God.'

'Sister, our time is up on the phone.'

'Will you write?'

'Yes.'

'When?'

'Tonight.'

'Write to her. God will tell you what to write.'

'Yes.'

'I will give your love to Bafemi. Should I wake him up? Can't they hold on . . . on the phone?'

'No.'

'All right. God will keep you . . . Tunji? Tunji!'

'Yes?'

'When will you come home?'

'Two years, or less.'

'Holidays?'

'I don't know.'

'God keep you.' She began his praise-song of *oriki* and as she sang plaintively, he called to her:

'Goodbye, sister.' She continued to sing. He put down the phone.

He looked at his watch. Fay said: 'You spent twenty minutes.' He grunted. His bill would be enormous.

That night there was no way he could escape the sublime effects of sentiment. His head rang with his sister's voice singing the oriki. He got up and dressed. He went out into the night, walking in the chilly north-easterly breeze. Fay went to bed. Tunji was determined to wipe out the sentiment; soothe it out, gently, so he could think and sleep. He made a circuit of his neighbourhood and went to bed at about two in the morning. He wrote in his diary that he would send a get-well card to Mary, and it would be the utmost of what he could do.

The Doctor with a capital D walked down the ward amid the enthusiastic greetings of the nurses. He was young, not yet thirty, brilliant and popular. The popularity did not stir him. It did not intrude into his devotion to his patients at the psychiatric ward. The feedback between the Doctor and his profession contained an assurance that only such people as healers could possess. Somehow, the Doctor did not have any presumptions, neither did he appear to be modest. He only did his work, as best as he could, loving it.

The young nurses referred to him among themselves as the Doctor with a capital D. He never became aware of the nurses' flirtations. He closed himself to them. He had not yet found out his own nickname and why he earned it with his good reputation.

The Doctor walked down the long ward, stopping to smile at the blank faces that lit up from the recesses of mental void. He called at an old lady who only recently had finally remembered her own name. He called a nurse's attention to the flower vase and asked for a fresh bouquet of flowers. He noticed a few beds on which slept some patients, apparently tranquillised. He frowned, and muttered 'If only it could be done without these drugs, stimulants and tranquillisers!'

He turned into a shorter corridor and went into the private room.

Mary sat up and smiled at him.

'Good morning, Doctor.'

'Morning, Mary.'

'When can I go home?' That was the question she had been asking for weeks. In the Doctor's opinion, he felt there was in fact no need to detain her any longer, but the regulations stipulated that patients were required to remain under observation, even after the signs of recovery were evident. The Doctor had pressed for her release while the senior medical officers demanded a strict obedience to the rules.

'Test her all over again. Run through the details of her family, her husband, the children, the letters and how they were ignored. Face her with her future; how she is to go out into the world as an unwanted wife. See how she takes it. Weigh up her chances of being married again and see if she can face another marriage without fear,' the Senior Medical Officer had said to the Doctor.

'But, doctor, I have done these over again.'

'You see,' the S.M.O. had continued to say. 'Fear is the element we deal with mostly in the illnesses of the mind. Fear and the instincts of self-preservation. Can you be certain that the fear is gone, that she can face another marriage without the horrors of this failed one lurking in the background? Can you be certain that she will not resort to this use of prayers as an opium? Can you be certain that she will make a proper use of her potential and relate herself to her God in a less parasitic way? Can you?'

'Yes.' The Doctor's answer was convincing.

'You see, we have had a case in which we thought the patient was all right until she got the offer of a second marriage. It was then we realised that our treatment had not ended. She suspected her suitor to a point of madness.'

'Let us take the risk, sir.'

'Risks? You do not expose some minds to risks, yet minds can mature in conditions of risks.'

'It is better than caging them up like this. It is simply not human.'

The Doctor's lips pursed as he realised that he should not have lost his temper. The Senior Medical Officer stared at him.

'I am sorry, sir. I should not have lost my temper. You see, sir, it should be possible to cure these illnesses without suppressing the activities we term "violence" nor should we violently activate the phase we see when they seem to be dormant. There should be a better therapy that is devoid of electric shocks, psychological shocks etc. etc., and sequestration should be abolished,'

'You should not be doctor. A priest – that would have been better. Do not involve yourself too much. It is because you are young in the profession. Patients are patients, there is no other term for them. Just as animals are animals. We need names to qualify things. You should accept the indignities of our therapy. They are part of the clinic. See to the patients, doctor. Let us run through our recovery therapy and observe her for another week.'

The Doctor had left the S.M.O.'s office, annoyed, and he did not bother to conceal his frown. The S.M.O. shook his head sympathetically after the young Doctor had gone out.

How could he, the Doctor, tell Mary what he had just gone through on her behalf, and on behalf of the other sick? He smiled.

'When will I go home, doctor' she asked again.

'In a week's time.'

'A week's time!' She jumped out of bed. 'This is ridiculous, doctor. You cannot keep me here for another week! Is this a joke? I have been here for seven months. Seven months in a hospital! Is this a jail? Let me go back to my family.'

'It's the orders.'

'Orders? Whose orders? I am going home, right now! Would you mind going out of the room while I change, doctor?'

He went out, smiling. He was delighted. She did not see his face. A few minutes later the door opened. He went in.

'I hope you realise what you are doing. There is a tight security here. Policemen and all.'

'I don't care. I am ready to live again, but not another seven days in this place.'

'You are right,' he said.

She caught the sincerity of his tone and stopped to control her fury, watching him.

'Mary, if you protest too much, they may regard your protests as symptoms. You have just exhibited clear traits of violence which will not help your cause.'

She sat down. His voice was appealing. As she listened, she began to remember how positively he had helped her on the road to recovery.

'Please co-operate. I promise that in seven days' time, with your co-operation, you will be allowed to leave.'

She protested again, this time, less vehemently. Finally, she said: 'It is absurd.' He could not agree more. She asked him to go out of the room while she changed back into her hospital clothes.

'Doctor, it is for my children that I have obeyed you and for the fact that you are nice and convincing. Otherwise, I would have given them trouble. Look, I have just become myself. I have been more or less dead for over two years. Seven days won't kill me. I'll stay.'

'Thank you, Mary.' The Doctor walked out.

Mary went to the balcony of the room and thought of what her father must have paid to have her in a private ward. She started to think of the Doctor.

Indeed it was he who guided her back to normal health, but if he was asked, he would say that the patient only recovered because she re-discovered the strength of her mind and body. He refused to accept praise. The doctor, he believed, only guided the patients. He had faced Mary on her first day in hospital, reduced her drugs to the minimum and begun the tedious task of discovering the key to her mind, because at that time, it was a mind whose owner had lost control. It only obeyed an automation that was given to it.

The Doctor reassured Mary's father and listened to the story of her background. He chose his keys from this background story and began to try them until finally one found an entrance. He revived her past and showed her her present. It was an enormous task. The patient took the Doctor as a friend and he won her confidence. Prayers he made into a small ritual in this therapy. In the third week, he allowed her to start the daily exercise with a prayer. It was a short passage that summarised her situation, stating that a man, her husband, had refused to continue with their marriage, for no reason. The prayer then said all she wanted was to have a marriage if it came, or live as a divorcee, if it did not come.

She was made to go through this piece of 'prayer' until in the fourth week, the door to the mind opened wider and she said she was ready to accept life in all its cycles. The Doctor became more encouraged and cut out the drugs. Slide projections of identical stories were shown to her, and gradually she came face to face with the reality of human cruelty and why it was necessary for her to see it as such, in all its meaning, and decide to use, in her particular case, the virtue of her religion.

The Doctor used everything at his disposal. Mary's mind became wearied of its immediate past of automation and realised the infinity of its own variety. From then on, the mind gathered strength as Mary sprang back to life, after a series of talks, tape-recordings, slide projections, visits by her parents, and faked letters from her children. During this latter part of the therapy she fully recognised the Doctor and liked him because of the tone of his voice, the touch of his hand, and his tirelessness of purpose.

'He helped me,' she said on the balcony. 'I'll be grateful to him forever.'

Seven days later, Mary went back home, on her own. The Doctor advised her to take a taxi, and not send for her father. She agreed and went courageously back to life.

Four

Mary's father sat in his usual position, bare from the waist up, looking on the street, watching the pedestrians make for home with the setting sun of dusk. His wife shouted from one of the inner rooms, asking for the time. He told her and then she said she was ready to go. She came into the room which looked on to the street and said to him: 'I'll hurry up so they don't close the hospital gates before I get there. Do you have any message for your daughter?'

'Tell her I send my love and I hope she will be back with us soon.'

At that moment Mary was drinking in the airy pleasure of health and freedom as she saw the town she had missed during her two years of despair and seven months of treatment. The northern garments of white shone in the sun of the dusk flowing in the plateau winds. A few coaches full of European tourists trooped past, one after the other. She realised that a new flower had burst in her, blossoming, reaching out to the sun of radiant health. As the taxi turned round the streets, her eyes caught a church building and then a mosque. She smiled and a prayer in Hausa escaped her lips; '*Nagode Allah.*'

She sat back, closed her eyes, longing for her children.

'Aren't you visiting her this week, then?'

'I'll wait till Saturday.'

'All right then, goodbye.' Mary's mother went out.

Mary's taxi came from a different direction and her mother had her back to it as she walked on briskly, so that the hospital gates would still be open when she got there. Mary did not see her mother among the other pedestrians.

Her father's eyes opened wide as he saw her get out

of the taxi, paying the fare. He dashed out of the room, still in his loincloth, and shouted in the direction which Mary's mother had taken. The taxi driver looked puzzled. Then in a flash he realised what the old man was about and offered to help, driving after the old woman.

Mary's father roared with laughter.

'It is my own May!' This was what he called her when he was pleased with himself or with her. 'It is my own May!'

Right on the street, he hugged her, unclasped his arms, held her away from him and hugged her again. 'My own May, child of Spring!'

His laughter rang throughout the street. Neighbours heard and called back cheering comments. He practically carried her inside. She was laughing too, raised high in joy, muttering: 'My own dear Father!'

Then her mother was racing home, tearing down the street, after the taxi driver had given her the news. Her wrap held tightly round her waist, her head-tie loosening and dropping to her shoulders, her very soul flying with exhilaration. Mary's mother tore down the street.

'Ayodele!' Mary called for her daughter.

'She is staying at your aunt's. We'll go for her tomorrow. With you in there, and your mother travelling endlessly to the south and me at work, I thought Ayo would be best at your aunt's.'

'You did well, Father.'

The door flew open and Mary's mother came in with the same force behind her elation.

'Ehn, ọmọ mi! Ọmọ mi Ajikẹ! Ọmọ ti ọla oluwa wẹ mọ, tio toro, nini, nini, nini. Ọmọ mi, ẹni iri Oluwa sẹ si le sẹ ki ẹsẹ ma wo, Ọmọ mi.

'Ehn, my child! My child Ajike! The child whom the Grace of God washed, my child who is clean, who is clean, who is pure, oh so pure! My child, on whose feet the dew of God sets, so they do not hurt! My child!'

The room was jubilating in oriki-song as Mary and her mother embraced each other, laughing, singing, sobbing all with joy. It did not matter then if she was an unwanted wife. It did not matter that she had had to fall ill to rediscover her vitality. Nothing else mattered that gathering dusk except this rejoicing family unit.

They all contained their joy with economy and Mary settled down. Her mother went to fetch Ayodele whose own joy could not be contained and would not be economised because like the child that she was, it was a thrilling emotion that she gave and took for the rest of the evening. When they retired to bed, very late at night, Ayodele slept close by her mother, asking her about her travels to the south for the child had been told that Mary had been on a trip to the south.

Two days later Mary's mother went to her shop, taking Ayodele with her. Mary stood under the lone mango tree in the backyard. Her father was oiling and putting some parts of his heavy motor-cycle in order.

'Thank you, Father, for all that you did.'

'You owe me nothing, daughter. Nothing. I had to do my duty or else what am I a father for?' He continued his work. 'I am glad you recovered completely. You should thank God in the church and have a *Saara*.'

'I have been thinking of it. I want my thanksgiving as a very special and quiet church service and I'll have a small Saara party for Ayodele and Bafemi. That, I hope, is as it should be.'

'Yes, daughter. A Saara is one's own private banquet for the whole perfect Ministry of the Father, thanking them. They have done their duty, we must do ours.'

'I am so happy. I'd like to start work again. I have been idle for three years of my life,' she chuckled.

Her father laughed too.

'I spoke to my friend at the Textile Mill. He thinks you could take a job as one of their clerical staff in two weeks' time. I'm seeing him tonight.'

'Thank you, Father.'

'It's my duty. Make sure you perform your duties rightly for your own children. No matter what.'

'Yes, I will, with joy and life.' She picked a dry mango leaf. 'I want to visit Bafemi at his aunt's place.'

'You should. I thought of it too. By the way, I kept your Post Office savings for you. It must have yielded interest. Tunji also sent some money for last Christmas for Bafemi and Ayo. I deposited that for you. He wrote to tell me that the children's insurance policy has been duly paid.'

Mary knelt beside her father, smiling. 'You have done everything so well, Father. Perhaps God knew the type of husband I would have, before he gave me to you as your only child.'

'Perhaps. The Old Man up there plans it so well for us. We are never to be defeated if we obey him.'

She rose and said: 'I'll take a seven-day trip to the south in two days' time. I'll take Ayo with me.'

'Good,' her father said. She went inside the house to start preparing his meal.

Her journey down south could not be similar to the journey up north, some years before. Going to the north then was a harrowing experience for her, emotionally. Then, the whole of her world was crumbling at her feet. This journey to the south was too slow for her, because her joy became too swift for the physical dimension of the moving train. She wished she was in Ibadan with her son Bafemi.

The savannah of the north gradually gave way to the rain forests after the River Niger had parted the land in its seaward journey. As the landscape changed its vegetation, so did Mary look eagerly towards her journey's end. After a night in the train and towards the close of another day, she arrived at Ibadan station.

Mary stepped into the street outside the station and her eyes caught the ancient and priceless market of Dugbe, its teeming thousands, its crawling traffic and the mixed glitter of the chrome of taxi-cabs and the glass panes of jutting skyscrapers.

A taxi pulled up beside her, as Ayodele looked about her excitedly. Mary headed for her sister-in-law's, where she was to stay for the seven days. Mama muttered endless praises for God when she saw Mary.

Mama had been afraid for her; would Mary still be

the same? Her doubts of medical science rose and fell. She expected hopefully a full physical recovery for Mary, but sometimes there came within her an overpowering sense of doubt, fearing that her sister-in-law might emerge with an impaired mental fitness. And so when Mary arrived with her daughter, Mama saw the spark of life in her eyes, the flash of fitness in her footsteps and as she spoke, it was with reason and assurance; Mama was so pleased that she danced in little steps singing that she would marry Jesus the Christ for ever.

Bafemi had gone for his art lesson that day, unaware of his mother's visit which had been kept from him as a pleasant surprise. Mary and Ayodele had a bath and changed into fresh clothes before having a meal. Night had completely appeared when Bafemi arrived with his art-kit.

This time, he stopped and looked at his mother, as the tiny cell of recognition began to enlarge in his memory, in a moment that passed very briefly. Then, he rushed at her. He dropped his kit, and held her to himself in extreme joy, with his sister tugging at his shorts, calling for an equal attention that she duly received.

On the sixth day, Mary went straight to the point. Bafemi had asked: 'How is Father? Do you hear from him? He sent me a big watercolour set.'

'Yes, I heard from your father, a long time ago, before I came to visit you last.' She watched him. He was a big boy now, grown to over five feet. In a few years to come, he would be in his adolescence, the doorstep to manhood. So, as she intended, without mincing words, she began to tell him the truth, the whole truth of her despair and illness. It was a quiet afternoon in the guava orchard that stood on one side of Mama's estate. Ayodele was out with Mama to a children's bazaar. Mother and son faced the facts alone.

Remarkably he listened without interruption. Then she finished: 'You are a big boy now, intelligent from what I have heard and seen. I know you will understand.'

Bafemi said: 'Woli tells me that there is always a reason behind an act. Nothing happens on its own, he says, everything has a reason behind it, be it good or bad. This is what Woli teaches me. Mother, why does Father not want you?'

'I don't know, Bafemi. I have tried to find out for some years. I ended up in hospital.'

The boy asked: 'Did you do anything to him, Mother?'

'No.' Mary said. They stood facing each other, without speaking. Then she continued: 'Your family is a fine one with a good reputation and with hard-working men and women. When I met your father, he was fine, ambitious and confident. Now he escapes my imagination. And I do not intend to pursue him any longer.'

'What will you do now, Mother?'

'I am going back to work next week. And I'll look after you and Ayo.'

'Will you marry again, Mother?'

She stood still. No one had posed her that question since she came out of hospital, neither had she been prepared to ask herself. She avoided the question in order to avoid plunging herself into thoughts. Then, her son looked up at her face, demanding an answer.

'Will you, Mother?'

'I don't know yet. I suppose I cannot stay at my parents for ever. I will not look for another man as an escape. I doubt if my whole love can come again, for another man.'

'Tell me "no" for an answer, Mother.'

Her heart beat faster. Her son imposed himself on her, jealously trying to keep her from anybody else apart from the original family unit. She could not blame him. The fact was that he had hardly known a home in which the two parents lived together. His father went to England when he was just emerging from infancy. He asked again and she realised to her horror that she could not give an answer, that she was incapable of giving the negative answer.

The boy could not understand why a negative answer

could not be given without hesitation. She realised that he was blameless. Anyone would keep what was his, lest it be snatched away. The home, the happy home of father and mother had never been his or his sister's. Never could there be replacement of the parental gem, even with the jewel of good relatives. The home was a gem to him and he sensed it going, but he was determined to retain it at all costs.

As his mother could not answer, he said: 'Please don't marry again, Mother, or we shall not be happy. If you do, I will never love you again, never!'

'Bafemi!'

'You will not marry again. My father will come back and we'll have a home, for ourselves. Say Amen, Mother.'

She laughed and said: 'Amen.'

That evening before going to bed, Bafemi prayed earnestly, feeling a snap somewhere in his mind, fearing that he was losing something too precious to miss, for which he would give anything to have back. Knowing that his mother was leaving the following day, he saw the picture of his home crack, break and turn into dust as his mind moved through a disturbing nightmare.

His mother felt no better, only she refused to brood. Yet already she feared that Bafemi would react disturbingly to the reality of the home she and Tunji had failed to give him and his sister.

She left for the north, physically refreshed, but sensing the disharmony that was being brought into the lives of her only children.

'Maybe a miracle will change things. Maybe.' That was her comment as she dared not build up other hopes. For her then, only the reality of the present mattered; that she was an unwanted wife, that her children had no home of their own and that this negative aspect of life had to be lived with.

Tunji got up from his desk just past one in the morning, and gulped in three full breaths. It was a Saturday evening and on the couch Fay was working on a collage, her favourite spare-time occupation. Tunji looked at her and said: 'Why don't you attend an evening course on the art of origami? You seem to be gifted that way.'

'Not after a blasted day in a factory. You know too well how this work breaks one down; all you feel like doing is going out and having fun. I lose my sense of concentration when I come out of that factory.'

'Keeping vigil with me then?'

'Why not? I want you to obtain your doctorate. You have worked very hard for it.'

'My mother and sister used to tell me a quote. I forget from where it is. It is something like: One who does not work should not eat. To them in the family work is a fulfilment, in all respects.'

'Not in a bloody factory.'

'They would argue for that too. If anything, that philosophy has stuck to me since infancy.' He searched for a distant station on the radio. Some strange voices cackled through the electronic whines. He switched off the radio and picked a Frank Sinatra long-play. In silence, they both watched the record roll to a start and the voice of the 'Ol' Blue Eyes' came on. He and she relaxed on their seats as one song came after the other, allowing the melodies to reach the recesses of their fatigued bodies. When the record came to an end, she got up.

'Sherry?'

'No thanks. My usual Cinzano Bianco, if you please.'

'Do you know, Toon-jie, somehow I don't want you to go home, but I know I can't stop you. I have known a few men, you know, as friends, and I have known you. In a way only you have drawn me to yourself, more through your attitude of . . . non-commitment. You do it so well that I want to wait on you all day.'

'I am not aware of it.'

'It is a very dangerous thing in you. This thing that is in your character could destroy any woman who gives too much for you.'

'Don't tell me I'm that negative.'

'I am a woman and I know what I am saying. Look at

it this way. Your ambitiousness is attractive because it's there in your eyes, the way you work and your single-mindedness. Your ... , shall we say, sociability is fantastic. At parties, don't you ever notice how many girls are drawn to you? Yet you appear unconcerned, uncommitted. Then your physique ... !'

'Are you determined to flatter me this morning?'

'No, it's absolutely true. I'm not flattering you, I'm just telling you how a magnetic personality like yours can be dangerous if you don't control it.'

'You amuse me.' He drank his wine in a gulp and rose to pour another one.

'I'm sorry for the woman who falls in love with you. Your brilliant career is assured, so is your material comfort, but how I wish Cupid would build a nest in your heart.'

He watched her keenly for a while and he put in: 'If I should study myself so well, my psyche and physique, then I would be on the way to the cult of personality-worship and that's dangerous. A man shouldn't be conscious of these things you mention. I'm guilty of only one thing and that's ambition, and even then it is my own constructive work to humanity.'

'What work is that?'

'My speciality is the home, the ideal rehabilitation of the home, with its natural environment in which man's mind and body will be at peace.' He smiled, pleased with himself. 'Did you ever climb to the top of the Post Office Tower in London, to dine at the restaurant? Have you ever cast a look at the city? What monster do you see? Long pillars of pigeon-holes for work and habitation; they are the products of your industrial civilisation. My people are still lucky. We have not gone too far. My ambition is to help re-plant the natural environment back home. This is more important than politics or materialism.'

She smiled. 'And it makes you feel like another Moses?'

He raised his eyebrows. 'Oh, not as far as that. The home, Fay, is the unit of the nation, and ideal homes give ideal nations.'

She laughed, betraying all the mockery that built up when he started to explain his mission. She laughed and swore: 'Bloody hell! It would have been better if men like you were not created. You are such a ridiculous waste of the nature that you want to rehabilitate!'

His face dropped and his eyes narrowed, not in anger, but in curiosity.

'You talk of homes! Do you have a home? What is the meaning of a home? Is it a physical architectural dimension to you? Or is it that centre-point of harmonious co-habitation? Jesus! How dare you give others homes when you have not built one for yourself?'

Her mockery rose with another laugh in the breaking-dawn of Sunday.

His inside became hollow as an emptiness welled up in him. He shut his eyes. He opened them again. He paced the room in short steps, each moment an effort to find his equilibrium again. When he felt better, Fay was looking at him with pity.

'Fay, you are right in a way, but what makes a man guilty when he decides he wants to become single again? You can't accuse me of breaking up a home when you have not even tried to build one.'

'I've never intended to. What made you go into it if you hadn't the guts to build it?'

'It is more than that, my dear Fay.'

'Toon-jie, one day you will face yourself in the mirror and ask yourself the question you have been evading. What makes a home? Morality of homes must surely be included in your project, or else it will fail like the tall pillars of pigeon-holes you condemn from the London Post Office Tower.'

'Being moral, eh? You should not have been my girl friend then.' He laughed, and his eyes changed to that lascivious come-to-bed glint. The wine had been flowing for a while in their blood.

He pulled Fay to her feet. 'Fay, you should go back to the university, you are too clever to be a drop-out.' They came together on their feet, hugging for a little while.

The heat of the argument subsided and desire rose from the bases of their spines. Tidal waves of passion mounted with the wine. They led each other to the bedroom, sinking into the bed when the dawn of the first day of week broke.

Five

Mama began to prepare Bafemi for secondary school. A year before his last year in the primary school she intensified her guidance over him. She often made reference to the secondary schools run specially by the Government. The boy not only studied arithmetic, and English to qualify him for admission, but also art, geography, history and civics were included in his curriculum. The Boy Scout movement was also an important part of Bafemi's spare time activities. He was encouraged to rise from tenderfoot to all the grades possible at his age.

It was therefore within the accepted code of conduct and the rules to allow him to go on a two-man camp, at the instigation of Bayo.

The artist and the boy apprentice had five days of forest camping ahead when they shut the door of the studio. Each had a bicycle, a big one for the artist and smaller one for the boy apprentice. Their minimum requirements were packed in mats, roped round in the fashion of nomads, and slung over their shoulders. They set out at dawn.

The artist chose a distance far enough out of town, and they rode out. The boy apprentice climbed up the hills, sped down the slopes, encountering the early palm-wine tappers on wheels.

They stopped to rest.

'I am tired,' Bafemi complained.

'Do you see the palm-wine tappers? Those boys are of your age.'

'They have been doing it for years.'

'Does Woli not tell you that strength is a fountain?'

'Only when it is economised. That's Woli's teaching.'

The artist saw a footpath and went into the

forest, leaving his apprentice behind. He re-emerged an hour later, when the boy was beginning to doubt the wisdom of the camp. The artist rolled his bicycle on and asked the boy to follow him. They went into the darkness and coolness of the forest. Outside, it was light and warm.

What was he doing this for and why did he obey this urge to come into this place, with the boy apprentice? The more Bayo searched for an answer, the less he found it possible to know. Since that night of the naked man at the Adept's and since his drunken exploration into the unknown woman's body, he had been keen on setting out; for where, for what, he did not know. He had two weeks' leave and he chose this camp. Originally he wanted to camp alone, but somehow he felt he should take the apprentice with him. It was easy to convince Mama, who was keen to see her nephew conquer the 'outward bound' course. Why had it seemed so easy even to make the Adept give his blessing?

The artist had doubts and fears and he determined to face up to them, once and for all. He remembered the smile of the Adept as he mused: '*Ohun ti a n wa lọ si Sókótọ, wa ni sòkòtò*', meaning that much labour was wasted in chasing what had been in one's possession all the time.

Disregarding the Adept's comment, the artist set out, taking his apprentice with him.

The child apprentice feared as they went deeper into the forest. The coolness did not soothe him, it crept under his skin. Walking behind the artist, he cast looks over his shoulders. Why was this necessary? Why did he have to go with this 'mad' cousin into this habitation of demons? Why? What was to be gained in this? Why did he have to do this when it was easier to go on the Boy Scouts' camp in a bigger company and have no fears of danger? The world of the African night closed about him. It was a nucleus of nights with outstretched limbs of the octopus twining, bursting, stretching, always describing the closing circle of the ancient tales. The forest was a reality to the boy apprentice. For the boy the tales merged fiction with reality, creating the dancing macabre shadows of the dark.

'Do not be afraid, Bafemi.'

It was as if the artist read the boy's mind. Even when it came, Bayo's voice only made Bafemi start, almost making him lose hold on his bicycle.

'We'll camp here.' The place was a clearing with overgrown grass. The artist took the cutlass and began to cut the grass very low. The apprentice, without being told, packed the grass to one side. He was instructed to leave it and let it dry, to form part of their nocturnal camp fires.

'You will enjoy it, Bafemi. I see doubts on your face. I am here with you and remember Woli's lessons. You are never alone.'

The boy smiled.

'That's my boy. There is a stream nearby. We'll draw our water from there, boil it, filter it with our clean white cloth and put alum in it. Remember, beauty is the focus of an artist's vocation. We have four hours to erect a tent. Our baths will be in the open. A hole, ten yards from here, will be our toilet. Over there are the low palm-trees. I'll cut the palm-fronds, you'll pack. I should tell you that we have a neighbour.'

The neighbour was the farmer who allowed the use of his land, for a fee of ten ₦aira for the week. Providence gave them a good start. It comforted Bafemi to know that a village was only two miles away. His mind settled gradually during the next four hours of work. The artist had the strength of the sculptor, the patience of the ceramist and the gentle hand of the painter, all of which aided the erection of their tent of palm-fronds, thickly roofed and walled, with an open door. The other white cloth draped the opening as a blind, and it was a sign of human habitation, in this forest of varied foliage.

Night closed in. Their bodies were fatigued. Their minds groped with doubts and the single question of

'Why did we come?' Their meal, a quickly boiled rice and mushroom soup with dry fish, was eaten as the nocturnal sounds of the African forests crept into their silences. The boy apprentice took his blanket, stretched himself on the thick *pakiti* mat that served as a bed, and slept.

When the artist made the fire with logs, twigs, and barks of wood, it was done as a necessity for warmth and as a subconscious need for a focus of meditation. As he sat down before this bonfire, his mind opened to a period of clear contemplation. The fatigue of the body was drained by the power of the mind, seeking contemplation. Yet the fear remained in forms of leaping shadows, groaning trees, squeaking bats, a thousand haunts of witches lurking in a fickle human imagination. The mind sought for the focus, refusing to cry out sharply in fear. The artist began to sweat. He wanted to get beyond the fear, and command these moments of stillness and movements. Climbing from the pit of fear to the peak of mastery was, on that night, an arduous task of slow seconds and sweat.

It was eccentric! Why did he have to come? Why seek this? For what?

His mind answered back in the voice of Woli as his contemplation assumed a bolder shape.

Long ago, he remembered, he sat in the Adept's garden, under a shade at noon, and they talked for a long while.

'Why do you keep running, Bayo? Why do you seek these shadows? Why do you ask these questions?'

'I want to know,' he said to the Adept. 'It must be possible to fulfil the divine in my art, never mind if I seem unworthy. Out of decay is rich manure. Why should the likes of me be unworthy, of the Grace, threatened by the Fear?'

'Sometimes I want to call you a name. It is Saul.'

'I haven't got the guts. I haven't got his courage to revolt to that point. I have one courage, though, to reject the fear, the basis of this Grace. It is nonsense, Woli, nonsense! How can we grasp the Grace with fear?

The fear of an eternal punishment. Why not have the Grace for its worth and not for the terrors?'

'And so you still revolt?'

'How?'

'By repeatedly shouting to the world how free you are, riding to the house of decadence?'

'No. I fulfil my God in my works. If I had the honour of a membership of the twelve, it would not displease me to be Thomas. That is why his face lives on my canvas.'

'You will wander back to the road, the only road.'

'I will tread no road whose milestones are inscribed by fear. I reject that road; totally, without compromise.' Bayo emphasised this, by waving his fore-finger in the air.

'The only road to the Grace has no fears. For centuries the so called teachers benefited from the fear of the masses, the cowering ones who panted under the weight of a false Grace. No, Bayo, there is only one way, and it is free of fear, its milestones are guidance. The barriers of altars will break and all shall be ONE, for One is the only beginning, that which reflects itself, indivisible, that which cannot be reduced, but multiplies itself to recur back to itself. One is the road. One is the Grace.'

The voice of Woli had been even on that afternoon, resonant, with its vowel sounds emphasising his points.

'It is for us to transcend the archetypes. Bayo, it is for us to know that our thoughts cannot be like the thoughts borne in the Grace for the Grace is not us and we cannot think like that which is not us. And the Grace is not fear. That is why the thoughts that bear fear are not the thoughts of the Grace.'

That afternoon the artist went back to his studio, to sit and stare at the perpetually emerging face of Thomas, that member of the twelve, who showed that to doubt was to ask for facts. It was not enough to be Thomas. It was the wholesomeness in knowledge that he sought, without the fear that distorted a thousand epistles and gospels.

Now, in the camp, Bayo remembered clearly the

voice of the Adept, as he gazed at the bonfire. He sighed and muttered, 'They use the fear as blackmail. I reject the blackmail.'

His mind gradually drained itself of all thoughts and the artist lost his awareness of the bonfire, of the bush, of the sounds, of the tent, without being conscious of any mental change. One thing took the place of the fire, and that thing was spherical and glowing in orange colour. This tiny sphere was like a magnified cell in its transparency. Then the body and the mind of the artist began to lose their awareness at a faster rate of vibrations until this human being became a cell being filled and swallowed up by the orange glow. The artist lost his selfhood in a transcendental surrender.

Within the orange glow, the human became part of the incandescence, without identity, without self-determination. The sphere hollowed itself into a vortex that spun with immense centrifugal force, with each of its million movements asserting itself in several scintillations. At the bottom of this vortex the human cell rediscovered itself and the artist felt the ecstatic delight of these flames, leaping as if from the bottom of a crucible burning the phoenix.

'There is only One road and it leads to the only consciousness. This is the cosmic consciousness.'

The artist heard the voice ride to him on the crest of endless echoes. The voice was Woli's.

'Do you not know that the Fear is merely the absence of the Grace? Do you not know that the dark is only the absence of light? Yet it is not for you to ask why the seed needs a dark sod to sprout from and to reach the sun. See? Does it begin to dawn that even the Crown needs the Kingdom for its reflection as the light fills up the nothingness of dark? That is the function of the Grace.'

The vortex went beyond any speed that could be measured. In a flash of transition the glow became growing shadows in which the artist saw his flesh and bones scale off in ashes, in processes of pain that gave forth strength. The falling off of the bones and the flesh happened rapidly in throes but left the artist with power. The darkness closed in and ringed him in a circle of gloom. As he looked up, he felt a pull, up the sphere, until he surfaced into a velvet nest of what turned out to be an opening rose.

It was then that light came.

The cell-incarnate enlarged into its form again. The delight of ecstasy fell. The mind and body came back to their own awareness in the weakness of birth.

Bayo looked about him. The night was very dark now. The fire was going out. He realised that a change had come over him. He stood up shaking his head, wondering if indeed he was still all right. He turned to the entrance of the tent.

There in the way was the form of the Adept, transparent. He turned his head in a direction and Bayo involuntarily looked that way. He saw a complete duplicate of himself, separating from him walking away, green with all the disgust and horrors of muck and decadence.

Bayo covered his face with his hands, his head reeling with fear, his voice rising in cries that only he could hear. 'No! Nooo! That is not me! That cannot be me! I am not that monster!'

The Duplicate turned and faced him and walked back towards him, in small steps. Each step brought an agonising groan from Bayo. The form that he claimed for his, was the pure form, the one that was glowing like Woli's form. Yet when the Duplicate moved nearer to him, the glow of his own form waned. He wanted to run, but a force rooted him to the spot. His cry of protest was pitched high, but its horror was so intensified that only he could hear it.

One step away from him, the Duplicate stopped. Its colours belonged to the spectrum, but they lacked brilliance and life. On its face was shame, contrition and a plea for life. It spoke: 'You have the past years to undo and then evolve a future. It is simple.'

Then it emerged with Bayo, its very source. The other apparition had gone. Bayo fell on his face in the most abject prostrate posture of shame.

Then he realised that it was his own apparition. It was his own self. It was his own psychic mirror that had no beauty to reflect. The Duplicate was merely the ugliness of the reflection from his own mirror.

That night contained many nights of experience. Bayo lay on the floor, and woke when the light of the sun filtered through the leaves in the morning. He kept silent in the present awe of self-recognition. Strangely, he was relaxed, expansive, but silent, determined to begin another act of self-knowledge. This, he felt, would be the most difficult, yet the best of all knowledge.

The child apprentice had his breakfast, wondering at how peaceful his master looked, how composed he seemed.

'I slept very well, Cousin Bayo.'

'So did I.'

'You got up before me. It's chilly in the forest early in the morning. I prefer staying in bed on chilly mornings.'

'You lazy drone, we have work to do.'

'What work?'

'Do you think we have come here for fishing and berry-picking? We are going to mix paints. There are many leaves in this place. We are to make many shades of colours, greens, blues from wild petals, indigo, red, brown, black. That's our first task. Work.'

They worked the whole day, picking leaves, soaking them, grinding them on stone surfaces, draining them of various shades of green, and an occasional red and violet. The work was done mostly in silence because the artist spent the time thinking of his new knowledge. 'Now I know,' he said to himself. 'The seed must taste the sod to know the sun. The vine must seek the soil to impregnate itself with the sun, in the grapes. Now I know.'

On the fourth day, Bafemi had the specimens of leaves pinned on paper, with the paint impression of the colours underneath.

'We look like herbalists,' he said to Bayo.

'And what's wrong with being one?'

'Nothing, if one will be like Woli.'

'Tell me, isn't your father coming home soon?'

'Yes. Mother said she will not go back to him because he does not want her.'

'And do you think he may change his mind?'

'He will have to change his mind, or I am not his son.' Bafemi looked up from his work. 'I will not live in the house in which my mother does not stay with my father.'

'That's too strong for a child to say, my dear apprentice.'

'I am not a child any more, cousin Bayo. Besides, we are all children in the face of God.'

'How very true. It seems you have been trained to know too much, a taboo for many children. It looks as if you will be a rebel before being the master.'

'I don't understand, Cousin Bayo.'

'You will, in a few years' time. Have you gained from this camp?'

The boy considered the question for a while, then said, 'Somehow I was afraid at the beginning because of the forest, but you have taken away my fear. Then, see the colours we are mixing. I did not know that so many colours existed in the forest. Why then do we buy the paints in the shops?'

'Being conventional, that's all. I'll take the specimens of leaves to the Adept and they will be identified. We'll do some paintings with the herbal colours for experiments.'

'Why did you come, Cousin Bayo? Was it for the herbal colours?'

The artist regarded his apprentice for a while. He went back to work. The boy stood there waiting for an answer.

'I suppose, in search of *Arodan*.'

'What is *Arodan*?'

'Ask Mama when we get back tomorrow.' Bayo grinned mischievously.

Self-knowledge could only be understood subjectively. Bayo would therefore not explain it to Bafemi. Self-knowledge would come to everyone in his own way, with his own cosmic force and through no one else. It would come, in spite of any efforts employed to prevent it. The boy apprentice needed nothing more than some guidance, this education, this experience he was receiving. The seed should not be forced, it would grow.

Arodan was what the elders sent the children searching for. The child in pursuit of *Arodan* ran many circles of errands that ended where he began. Within the orbits of human stupidity, each man went in pursuit of *Arodan*, hoping to fulfil his aim in his own selfishness, until his existence was betrayed by his own futile efforts.

Bayo knew then that he had been in search of this *Arodan*, even as far as the forest. But he had found it, as everyone eventually would. *Arodan* is ignorance revealed through an awareness, for a new beginning.

By dusk the theme of a new painting became strong in his head. Its title would be *Ecstasy in Arodan*.

Master and apprentice left the forest on the fifth day, the apprentice knowing the splendour in the wild foliage which had yielded so many colours, rejoicing in his new knowledge of the seeds and berries, crushed, ground, cycled in many processes to give the hues for new experiments in painting. He was glad of this new knowledge, marvelling at the brilliance of his master.

The master was at peace. Peace was a feeling he had missed for years. He felt wiser, knew why, but kept silent. At the exit of the forest, he looked back wondering at the many existences of the little universe, vowing to own his self-knowledge and relate it to a greater cosmic one.

He prayed in his mind for the apprentice. If, and when, his father came back, the edifice of the apprentice would be tried by many billows of emotions. Would the edifice stand? It was clear that Bafemi would reject the vulgarity which Bayo was certain would surround his new home in the name of a sophisticated life.

He hoped for the best for his apprentice.

They rode back to town, both of them the wiser.

Six

Bafemi's father, Dr Tunji Sotomi, was returning home. Curiously, it aroused no excitement in Bafemi. Instead, his subconscious decided to build up its battering-ram of attack and defence against this man who had rejected his mother, a legitimate wife.

Obviously, Dr Tunji Sotomi was a very important personality. The mass media telegraphed, telecast, broadcast, and teleprinted his name and pictures. The family required little to effect the usual ostentatious welcome-back-home ceremonies for their long travelled child. Society liked the homecoming reception to be held with all the glitter, fake and genuine, that borrowed money could buy. So some families did what society wanted, and advertised it in the papers, in the usual two-dimensional pattern; a photograph, the name of the returning self-exile, a list of his accumulated diplomas, certificates from the known and obscure institutions of Europe and America. The heading was always 'Advertiser's Announcement'. The people did not accept the maxim of refusing to blow one's own trumpet. On the contrary, they recommended a powerful trumpet, implying 'friend blow your trumpet, loud and clear'. Sadly enough each succeeding family was bent on outdoing the other families mainly at the expense of their pockets.

Fortunately for Dr Tunji Sotomi, his family did not need to incur that usual wastage. The Exe Company of Environment, Nigeria Limited, had to publicise his experience, genius and homecoming in respect of their profitable commercial goal. As was his habit, he ignored the publicity, set his mind only on his goal, confident of success. The effect was that within a short while, his charisma had grown. The initial period of return was spent on his work and the simultaneous rehabilitation of himself. His staff enjoyed working with him, reflected on his taste for fashion and his quiet strength.

Mary heard all about Tunji's return. She made a phone call to him and all he said were casual greetings. She went straight to the point.

He commented: 'Mary, I'm sorry if it seems unacceptable. I am simply not suited to marriage. I made a mistake in the first place. The children are taken care of. And I wish you would not raise the subject again.'

She paused painfully: 'All right then. I suppose it is the imprint of England on your character.'

'No, Mary. England has nothing to do with it. I'd like to have the legalities sorted out, ... you know without any fuss.'

'You make it sound civilised. I have made up my mind not to press you any further. It's been long enough to build up strength for your verdict. The children will sooner or later ask you why. May God bless them – ' She paused and breathed heavily, then asked: 'Tunji, can I just see you? Can I come down to the south, just for a personal contact, to talk things over?'

'That's very risky.'

'Maybe you'll change your mind?'

'No. Capital No.'

'Right' – pause, cough – 'It's no use my crying, anyhow. What are your plans for the kids?'

'Bafemi will come and live with me. I'll send for Ayo later if you do not object.'

'No. They hardly know you now. I hardly do either.'

'All right, Mary ...'

There was an uneasy silence between them.

'All right, Tunji ... God bless ... ' She hung up quickly. She sobbed quietly. Afterwards, she wiped her eyes, determined not to have any more emotional problems. 'And there I am, the unwanted wife,' she said to herself in self-mockery.

Tunji leaned back in the chair after the phone call. He decided to give her a good monthly allowance to re-settle her. On his decision, there could be no turning back.

'I will be an out and out bachelor.'

He went back to work. He buzzed for his secretary. 'Have you heard from the rest of the interview panel?'

'Yes, Dr Sotomi.'

'As I said, I don't want to see the names of those shortlisted. Send me the typescripts of their experience, marked by their initials.'

'Yes, Dr Sotomi. Any coffee, sir?'

'No. Not in this weather. I'll go out for lunch.'

Tunji studied the project map on the wall of his office. There were three villages marked out for the new environment scheme. He marked them as the first triangle. The first village was between Abeokuta and Lagos, the second village between Ibadan and Oshogbo, the third village on the far side of the Ekiti province, bordering their Edo brothers of the mid-west. He made notes and later put the finishing touches to his touring plan. His secretary entered with the list of short-listed applicants, two of whom were to be chosen for employment in the firm. He spent the next hour studying the typescripts of the applicants.

Shortly before break he reached for his own copy of his thesis, leafed through and found the page he wanted. He read it and made mental notes.

'The thesis is theoretical, mainly speculative but rooted in facts. Now I have the reality. This is my baby, as the Americans would say. This firm is my baby.'

Tunji went out for lunch. He went down the stairs, avoiding the lift. He went down four floors, in a determined effort to prevent the corpulence of tech-nocrats. He got into the Range Rover, drove to the Tennis Club.

Mope was a telephonist at the club who for some days had been hoping to get to know Tunji in spite of his aloofness. She read into his nature a debonair reckless-ness, from which she hoped to profit. Mope had designs upon him and the confidence to accomplish them. Without knowing it, Tunji Sotomi became one of her designs the moment she set eyes on him.

He had a favourite meal of three *moin-moin elemi meje*,

and a cold bottle of maltex. He reached for a cigarette. A tender female had offered one, from an angle behind him.

'Being generous, are you?'

'Yes, why not, to a man who eats here often and seems too reluctant to say hello.'

He accepted her cigarette.

'Ah, don't be misled. I am only engrossed in a project at the moment. I am not a misogynist. On the contrary ...'

'You are a Casanova.'

'No. Wrong again. I am a man, a normal man of today. You know, I have my tastes mixed with some delightful vices.'

'Which always seem to be well timed and organised. You have just come back?'

'From where?'

'Abroad.'

'Why? Do you notice anything?'

'Your mixed accent. And your face ... That's it! Sotomi! Dr Tunji Sotomi.'

'And you?'

'Mope. Just call me Mope.'

She had a drink on him. He then tried to determine her. This was the new generation. The young women who reached out without inhibition. Sophistication was part of their armoury of self-determination. Their attire was a blend of the 'Afro' and the imported look. On the whole, Mope was a trendy girl of twenty-two. Physically, she looked slim and long-legged in her clogs, which Tunji took for shoes.

Over the drink, she did more of the talking. She was a telephonist on a temporary basis. She intended to go to the polytechnic for a secretarial course. She loved parties and was on a slimming diet. He said nothing much about his job. Then she pressed further:

'Do you come to the Tennis Club in the evenings?'

'No. I go to a small Lebanese club in town.'

'The Mahharani?'

'Yes. Not regularly, though. Do you want to come along next Friday?'

'Yes. Why not?'

'I'll see you then; over lunch tomorrow. Thanks for the cigarette, Mope. I feel like taking you to several other clubs ... but I am a busy man just now – going on tour for the next three months, in and out of Ibadan.'

'Oh yes? That sounds nice.'

They left each other.

He drove back to the office through the Ring Road. He was remembering Fay, who had gone back to the university before he left England, after practically living with him for the last two months of his stay abroad. As the English girl herself said, he did not know her. There was nothing much to remember about her except her experimental cuisine, and their bodies, locked nakedly together in lustful consummation. He entered his office and dismissed the thoughts of both Fay and Mope from his mind.

But Mope did not dismiss him from her mind. Back on the switchboard, she rang a friend.

'Sadia, I've caught a fish! You'd be surprised. Somewhat of a well-known figure, a brilliant professional man.'

'Tell me, tell me you lucky devil ... What will you do with your sugar daddy?'

'He's a dirty old man. I am tired of him. My new catch is youngish, you know, thirty-ish. I like him. We're going out on Friday, first date.'

'Tell me his name.'

'Not yet. Top secret ... Sadia, I'll call you later, someone is trying to get through on the switchboard.'

Many calls came through that afternoon. Between them, Mope planned her next move. She was going to do what she had done to other men, look into their star trends to find out their strengths and weaknesses, plan how she would utilise the planetary indications to her own ends. Her consultant was an old man, called Baba Ake, who knew the art of reading the oracles, and like many of his kind, used this art diligently.

Mope never saw any other way to plan, to solve a

problem, than to resort to the use of oracles, to which her late mother had also been addicted.

Later in the afternoon, she intended to take Tunji's name to Baba Ake for consultation. Recently too, she had been secretly hoping to get herself settled with any prosperous young man, by any means available to her. True to her background, she had recourse always to the oracle, as her mother did before her.

Already Mope was scheming to get Tunji for herself. Tunji did not think of her at his work. He usually did not think of women, when working.

Bafemi stood before Mama. She had a letter in her hand. Since his return from abroad, Tunji had been touring and interviewing people, mostly away from home. Now, he wanted Bafemi to come and live with him. The boy received the news with mixed feelings, wondering if it meant going to the home paradise that his imagination built up, or if it was the false home that his instinct warned him of. His father wanted him home at the end of the school term three months away.

The other troublesome feeling was the imminent departure from Mama. It appeared to him that he would lose everything, including the art lessons, and visits to Daniel, the Adept.

'Will I be able to go for the art lessons?'

'Yes, your father should allow you to.'

'And will he let me visit Woli?'

'I should think so too.'

Bafemi said nothing for a while. A lump had built up in the middle of his chest, as he struggled to bring out the vital question:

'Will my mother be there?'

'No.'

'I am not going!'

His protest and anger came to the feverish heights that had been built up during the past months by his nervous speculations.

'I am not leaving, Ma! I want to live only with my father *and* my mother . . . I am not going to live with him

67

alone, without my mother!'

'Your father wants you to come and stay with him. He loves you. He's your father. You have been here for nearly six years. Don't you want to live with your father?'

He began to cry in violent bursts. His refusal was apparent. Mama folded the letter back. She brought the boy closer to her and hugged him affectionately.

'You are a big boy now, Bafemi. Do not cry. You are not going to a stranger. It's your own father.' She stroked his head and wiped his tears. 'I have taught you to be strong, to be good. Remember, Woli has told you to be fearless. If you're strong, fearless, and good, you will not cry.' She rocked him gently.

How was he to know that she loved him too, as a mother would love a son? Her pride lay in seeing him grow from moment to moment, his character being moulded. He was her ideal of a fine young man. She hoped that Tunji would provide all that the boy needed, morally and materially.

'Don't cry, Bafemi. I'll come and visit you. You will also call on me at weekends. It is the same town, you know. You are not going away from Ibadan. You'll still be in the same town. Now, be quiet. What do you want people to say, seeing a big boy like you crying?'

He stopped sobbing.

'Mama, why must I go if I don't want to? Can he not come and visit me? Then I'll go when I feel like it.'

She smiled. 'No, Bafemi, that is not right. Let your father have you if he wants to see you grow up in his house. Remember that if he had not gone to England, you would be with him now. You would never have been brought here. You know that the authority of parents is ordained by God. So you'll be good?'

Slowly he nodded his head. It was the mention of the divine authority that broke his resistance. He was not yet bad enough to resist when he heard the mention of the name of God. This was part of the consequence of his background. At Mama's wish, he slowly left the room, experiencing the oppression of an authority that he felt was arbitrary.

In the evening, he did not go to sleep early. Insomnia granted him the pain of thinking and questioning, for the first time in his life, the divine authority. Why should he be made to go back to a father he instinctively hated? No matter what premise he employed for this debate, he was perpetually losing. The child, Bafemi, had an urge to resist, but he lacked the courage. An immense fear of the consequence of any rebellious act swelled in his chest and choked him. The fear was of man and God. He was a child, but he felt the terror of oppression, the impotence of his revolt. Tears weakened him and finally brought him well-earned sleep.

He walked along the reeds that crackled against his heavy boots. He marvelled at the wealth of the soil, the experience of the ancient hands that tilled it and the possible breakthrough of the new commune. Why was the Old Baba from Odo-Ode still resisting? Why? Tunji had revealed every plan to him. Nothing was disrupting the old communal structure. Wealth was to be added to it in a new way of self-sufficiency. The sunlight was to supply the solar energy that would generate the powerful livewire of the community. The soil would yield again. Yet the Old Baba hesitated, having held the contract forms in his possession for weeks.

This was a laboratory for the environmentalist. This village, like the satellite villages of this vast continent held the source of life right in the soil. This the Old Baba knew and for this he waited for time. Tunji Sotomi climbed the hill and stopped at the top, holding the binoculars to his eyes, surveying the acres of vegetation. In him was the rush of ambition to turn Odo-Ode into the commune, the self-regenerative unit of human existence, free of the neuroses of the city, rich in harvests of health and creative longevity. He brought out his plan and went through the graphic sequences.

It was a gift he was bringing to these people. It was no exploitation. E.C.E. was self-sufficient in its architectural ventures. However, Tunji knew the value of standing out of the throng of designers and creating a new programme. The commune was not new in its essence. No group could claim monopoly of its creation. Why? The commune was created by nature, when the first man got his food from the soil. Methods were the only factors that could be put in dates. The commune was ageless.

He turned on the boulder and went down the slope. He stopped, turned round and saw her.

There she stood resplendent in some grace at once soft and fierce. She looked him in the eyes, not submissively, but commandingly. There was no make-up on her face, nor was she wearing any jewellery. Her attire of local indigo-blue enhanced her light complexion.

'Dr Sotomi?'

'Yes, that's right. Have you been following me?'

She laughed. 'Yes, why not? I decided not to go to the Rest House twenty miles away. I told someone to keep an eye on you when you came here again.'

'Why? Who are you?'

'Sulola. I belong to Odo-Ode, but I live in Ibadan. I am a contractor, a building contractor, among other things. Exporter, importer, etc. I know all about you. I mean, about your job, and I want to help you.'

He regarded her for a while. She was aware of his effort to control the situation. She did not yield. She kept her eyes on him.

'Dr Sotomi, I see that you love the village. You love it dearly. Or is is an infatuation?'

'No. It is genuine. How does one explain the be-all and end-all of one's existence?'

'When that happens, it is usually love; being in love with a job, a woman, or even God. When one feels like you do, it is genuine. Dr Sotomi, I want to talk business.'

'Here, or back in the Rest House?'

'Here, in my cottage. Besides, the young lady at the Rest House may not take kindly to seeing me.'

'It has nothing to do with her.'

'She is your girl-friend or mistress, is she not? Women are jealous, even mistresses.'

She led the way. He followed in earnest, feeling instantly obliged to her. Sulola was not fat. She was lithe and therefore light of foot. The agility of her gait showed a pronounced physical strength. Strangely, he admired her, but took it off his mind. The business mattered first.

They sat in the large living-room of the cottage. She served him some roasted bush meat and offered him palm-wine. She was relaxed. Her hospitality showed that the subject of their meeting was not to be discussed until the meal and the drink were taken. It only disarmed one. Abroad he was used to business luncheons being held with the discussion in progress. Sulola entertained her guest before allowing anything to be said. The expansiveness of the atmosphere made time stand still, disarming the guest.

'The Old Baba is my uncle.' She went straight to the point as a maid cleared the low stools of the left-overs of roast meat. 'He does not trust you young men. I don't blame him. He does not trust even his own young men, when they have stayed too long in the city. He believes that the city contaminates youth and I do too. There is no sincerity in the craving for money over there.'

She held him with her eyes. He took her gaze with calm. Vaguely, she felt a liking for him, but her thoughts did not disturb her expression. She took some palm-wine.

She continued: 'What can an old man say again when one after the other the city has betrayed him through many hopeless schemes. First the colonialists, then the politicians. He said to me yesterday that now it is people like you who will pounce next, the business tycoons. I agree with him. It is as if the soil did not build the nation before the oil came. The betrayal of the villages is evident. Do you disagree, Dr Sotomi?'

'No, but I am not a politician. I am not a business-man. I am an environmentalist.'

'You are a business-man. You are doing it for money.

What car do you drive?'

'Range Rover.'

'Mm, it makes little difference. It is still a vehicle that not everyone can afford. The only thing is that you are unique.'

His heart jumped for joy. For the first time, there was a smile of approval on her face. She saw the glint of confidence in him. She continued: 'In England, or wherever you stayed abroad, you used a car, no?'

'That has nothing to do with it. It was a necessity.'

'Dr Sotomi, you have not suffered.' Her voice was stern. 'You do not know how much these villages believe in the soil, the farms, the cocoa, our golden pod. You do not know how it feels to see the money you give through the soil being used by the thieves in the city. You do not know how it feels when, one after the other, the programmes succeed and you receive no returns. If those men remaining were not old, they would substitute guns for hoes and matchets.'

She pierced him with her look.

'Yet I tell Old Baba that our self-help funds should be spent on artisanal and agricultural developments. We do not want the industries here; neither do we want to fight in arms. The new era of self-help funds is working, but we fear betrayal from the cities.'

The project of the new commune fascinated her. It meant recalling the agricultural essence of Odo-Ode. It delighted her too to cut off any dependence on the city. She saw in the Solar Power Unit a complete serverance with the city. Tunji explained further that the electric lines indeed represented the lineal umbilical cords with the city. The water pipes represented the same lineal arrangement. It not only made rural existence dependent, it also exploited the old villages. Rates were paid, in return for little services.

The environment expert explained: 'We'll give you the energy. It comes from the sun which belongs to God. We'll rebuild the village in a farm commune, in a position which will favour the use of streams of air. Air belongs to God. We'll recycle your drainage and use the solar power to redam your river. If God demands tax for the sun, you have your religion to use in his worship. Artisans will rise again, not to be exploited, but to work for the commune. Your cocoa pod, your palm-oil, your forests will yield at the price you want.'

She asked if there would be no tax to be paid on the new electricity. He explained that collective tax would be worked out and the normal tax on the mechanical plant for the solar unit be paid. There would be no bills and everlasting power-cuts because of endless strikes, the chronic disease of city employees and their employers.

She sat back and closed her eyes. There were communes in some other places. They existed through small-scale industry, and they were morally knit through some religion. Odo-Ode was to be planned on the lines of an agricultural commune. Would it work? Why not?

'You will retain the farming structure. Don't you want to save the old farms? Don't you want to recall the young men? Do you want the tycoons to buy the land and become farming magnates? Don't you know that your acceptance will be an example to the rest of the nation? Sulola, help save the farms, or the people will starve. We have had enough of the industries. We need food. The farms are dying.'

She got up from her chair, lit a cigarette. She looked out of the window. The land stretched out in brown and green. A few mud houses lay on the green, mostly in circles. The house of the Bale was in the centre.

'This nation will starve if the farms are not saved. Villages like this one will die.' She turned to him. 'I am very proud of where I come from. Yet it annoys me to see that if I decide to come and live here for a year, I may end up in poverty. I come anyway, I come for the weekends.'

'Like most successful people. It is a shame.'

'Yes it is. Where do you gain from it?'

It was his Ph.D. thesis he was putting into practice. He told her of the kibbutzim he had studied from the angle of the architect and enviroment expert. He told her of how, even abroad, he saw people experiment with the commune. The commune had belonged to his nation, it had been looked upon as primitive, mainly because of the absence of power supplies and sanitation.

'My company will have to be paid the fees for the development. We know the villages can afford it.'

'How?'

'We have banking facilities made available from abroad.'

'Loans?'

'Yes. Paid back through the years.'

She did not like it.

'What if we pay thrice, raising funds through the self-help project. Once we start, we'll receive funds. Once the harvests begin to yield, we'll be richer. Five years of risk. Do you accept that?'

'If the first payment is made available. The set-up is cheap, Sulola. This is not a million-dollar project. We gain through the establishment of several others, here and abroad, where agriculture is the mainstay of the economy.'

She asked him to come and see the Old Baba. They left her cottage and went to the Old Baba. The conversation was brief. He would send his answer to Dr Sotomi at the Rest House the following morning. Tunji went back to the cottage with Sulola and thanked her.

'Don't thank me, Dr Sotomi. Let's hope for the best.'

'Meet me over breakfast in the morning. I'll send the car.'

'I'll come. I have a car. A Mercedes. The garage is right inside the village.'

He left. He felt happy and anticipated a positive answer from the Old Baba. He began to think of Sulola as he drove back. Her strong character was evident. She was his match. It dawned on him that it finally seemed possible for his mind to open towards another woman, for the reason that she was a woman of strength and independent spirit. The business negotiation made him feel like seeing her again, taking her out. It was funny to recall how Mope, the young telephonist, had got into this trip. Somehow she had managed to get him to take her along. Each night when he went to bed, puzzled and troubled by Old Baba's hesitation, Mope was there to give him her wild passions of the flesh, until they were both spent in each other's sweat. He felt only a physical attraction to her. It was nothing compared with this new longing for Sulola, not only in flesh, but in spirit. Without his knowing it, he was already mentally prepared to see her on the following morning.

When Mope made advances towards him in the night, he turned away gently. He did not need her.

Mope did not sleep early. She ran over the scheme in her mind. Within the last fortnight she had discovered that she was pregnant. It made her happy, like the gambler whose stakes finally brought in the jackpot. She would become his woman, his wife. She would resign from her job and be his housewife, with all his money. She would make him buy a car for her and make him send her on summer flights to Europe or America for shopping. She would become a grand hostess for his dinner parties, luncheons and even banquets. She became, in her imagination, a little madam, surrounded by the plush of success. She was glad that she was pregnant for Tunji Sotomi.

He was up early in the morning. He put on his best casuals. Mope rang the reception of the Rest House and asked for her breakfast in bed. Tunji mentioned nothing special about his breakfast. It simply was a breakfast with a business associate from the village. He said nothing to Mope. He had never said much about his work to her.

'Darling, I'll have my bath in time, and then you can take me to the village.'

'It's not a tourist session, Mope. Anyhow, I'll see you later.'

She shrugged her shoulders indolently.

He went out to the lounge. Sulola arrived in her Mercedes. She came in with a brief-case. They greeted each other and went to the breakfast table. They had breakfast over talks that had little relevance to the contract. Before long, she knew that he admired her. It was in his eyes. In spite of his efforts to concentrate on the conversation, she saw his desire. She had nothing against it.

They were having coffee when she spoke of the contract.

'My uncle has signed the contract. Yesterday they performed a ritual ceremony over it. You came at the right time. It was the new moon yesterday evening.'

He put his hands over hers. 'Thank you, Sulola. My company will start working right away.'

'Don't thank me, Tunji.' It was the first time she had used his first name. 'If that project fails, you'd be damned.' She laughed. He laughed too.

'It will succeed. It will. By the way, Sulola, I'd like to take you out in Ibadan, to celebrate. Do you object?'

'No. Not to a hard-working and attractive man. Your wife is a lucky woman, except she must not know about the little mistress on tour with you.'

'I am not married any more. I, er, decided to give up marriage. It has too many strains and trappings. I have two kids, a boy and a girl. And I don't intend to get married again. I should have my divorce sorted out soon.'

'You are weak, I am sorry to say. But I am frank with myself and with people. We all have our weaknesses anyway.'

'Are you single?'

'Yes. And I intend to remain so. I had two sons by two different men. The sons died very young. After that I decided I would have no more of male oppression. Look, Tunji, I must go. Here's my card.'

They went out. He accompanied her to the car. She stopped and turned round.

'Your girl-friend is stabbing me with her gaze.'

Tunji looked towards his suite which overlooked his parking space. There on the balcony, Mope stood staring with feline eyes, in which her anger and jealousy clearly showed. Tunji turned away. Sulola climbed into the car.

'The more she hates me, the more I may like you, Tunji. That's a dangerous female. I know one when I see one. I'll see you in Ibadan.'

She drove off, smiling.

Tunji strode back to his suite, holding the contract papers. Mope was still on the balcony. He ignored her and rang his office in Ibadan, giving the London representative of the firm the good news. He packed his papers; and informed the reception that he was checking out. He asked Mope to pack up as they were going back to Ibadan. She was sullen. He took no notice of her. He had decided to drop her at her place, back in town, removing her from his life completely. They left the Rest House within thirty minutes, heading for home.

'You should have said that it was to delight that bitch that you went to the village, instead of telling me lies about an old Baba. She is the queen of them all, the ruthless D-madams.' Mope gave a scornful laugh. 'If you go after her, you'll be ruined.'

'That's my business. It has nothing to do with you. You have no claim on me. You're not special to me, in any way.'

'I see. You should have said that before bringing me along for three weeks in a Rest House. As for having no claim on you, you are wrong. I am pregnant!'

The disclosure made him hold tight to the steering wheel. Then he relaxed and said: 'It makes no difference. You'll have an abortion. It is still young, if it is true.'

'Of course it is true! I have been here with you long enough for it to happen!'

'All right, all right. You'll have an abortion.'

'Is it as simple as that?'

'Why not? I do not wish to be your husband,' he said with finality.

Mope said nothing for a while. Then she spoke again, bitterly.

'You will be the father of my child anyway. I will not

have an abortion! You will have to accept responsibility for me and the child, even if it means living with you as a wife. What did you take me for? A prostitute? I won't be used, Tunji, not by any man. You shall father my child!'

The tone of her voice sent shock waves down his spine. Momentarily he lost his confidence. The situation became tougher when he cast a glance at her. She was determined. The fact was grimly imprinted on her face. He drove on in an uneasy silence, thinking of nothing because he was incapable of clear thoughts at that moment.

Seven

It was not necessary to regard 'juju' as the supernatural – this was part of Baba Ake's explanation to Mope. Neither was it necessary to tremble at the fear of spells. Only the rule of suggestion and association had to be observed. A man would not be affected by a spell without any association with its source, and the suggestive instinct of his mind. Baba Ake believed that he harmed no one, neither did he cheat his clients. There were clients who came back complaining that the juju he made for them was ineffectual. He retorted always by reminding them of the rule of suggestion and association.

'Perhaps, your subject does not believe in juju. Perhaps you have no justifiable association with him. Perhaps you have not dealt with him and the oracle in fairness.'

Baba Ake insisted on a just cause and reason from his client. Those who came back disappointed, and these were many, he asked to re-examine themselves. Once he told an insistent man: 'I will not kill for you. Go to witches or other horrible cults for that. What I carry out is justice. A man is cheated. I help him get back what is his. A woman's child is killed by a witch, I make sure the witch pays with her life. I deal in justice.'

Baba Ake had a clear conscience when he was at his work. He refused the notion of endlessly waiting for the gods to interfere on behalf of human victims. He believed firmly in petitioning the gods, bribing them, and making them enforce justice, immediately. He belonged to a powerful cult of similar men. They believed in their processes and fattened on their conscience.

It was to Baba Ake that Mope took her case. She was pregnant, she said, and the father was refusing to let the baby live. The man did not want her, because of another woman. Mope wanted to have her child for this man. She wanted to live with this man, as a child-bearing wife should, well taken care of.

Baba Ake asked her for a coin of any value. She put it on her forehead, as instructed. Thus surrendering herself to the oracle, she gave the coin back to him. He put it in the fine white sand, smoothed the sand over. Gently he began to read the oracle, touching the sand here and there, as it was done ages back.

Mope watched him.

'You are telling the truth, child. You are pregnant. It will be a son. It is now going to a month. This man you talk about has a royal sign. That is very interesting. He is a brilliant man, a leader in his field, determined and always doing things his way, in the manner of kings. Mmm.'

He touched the sand several times again. 'He is married or, shall we say, separated. There is still uncertainty about that. Mmm ... He has a son and a daughter. And the other woman you refer to is like the man; she has a royal sign, the same characteristics. However, what matters to you is yourself ...'

Baba Ake gave his verdict shortly afterwards. He would help her. The man in question would take her into the house. There was a very strong tie between them. It was the foetus. The spirit of the unborn would make him bring her in. There, the powers were in her favour. She was warned of her aggressive tendencies, her temper and loose tongue.

'A king does not like insults. He wants things done his way. My child, that is all.'

'Baba Ake, what about the woman?'

'What about her? She has done you no harm. I cannot hurt her for you. All I can do is give you a small ingredient which makes your man want you more than her. That you must agree will be ill timed since you are pregnant.'

'Can't you make sure he does not leave me for her?'

'She is not marrying him. Have no fears about that.'

Baba Ake's fees of forty ₦aira were paid. She went home expecting results. Baba Ake went back to work, singing to himself, thoroughly enjoying his duty.

Bafemi went back to his father's home as if he was going into the unknown. He had never as a growing boy lived long with his father. On the day of his departure from Mama's he felt so sad that he lost his appetite and vomited what he had tried to force himself to eat.

'Honour thy father and thy mother.' . . . That was the commandment being drummed into his head for days. Nobody listened to his protests. Mama felt the change was necessary for him to prevent a complete alienation between father and son. Bayo told him that it was necessary for him to live with his own father, according to the tradition. Woli reminded him of God's guidance wherever he would be.

Bafemi had no alternative. He went into an unknown future. His father's house was a designer's dream. It was dome-shaped, a special design by Tunji Sotomi himself. The wonder and splendour of the gardens outside the home captured the boy's aesthetic fancy. His small portmanteau in hand, he surveyed the layout of grass and flowers. The air was filled with the delicate scent of petals. Bafemi's resistance to the home lessened. He climbed the stairs to the entrance and pressed the bell.

The houseboy opened the door and said that he was expected. Bafemi insisted on carrying his portmanteau. If the outside of the dome was of splendour, the interior of the house was a marvel. The daylight was bright. Bafemi looked up and saw the sky. The ceiling and the roof were transparent and light came through losing its heat on the way. The boy was to learn that the heat was recycled for household chores. The coolness of the house was not the result of any air-conditioning machine. It was its natural position to air-streams, as Bafemi was to learn later. There were no automatic doors. All doors opened normally. The furniture was a rich blend of oriental and African craftsmanship. The house charmed the boy's spirit. He livened up.

The houseboy led Bafemi to his room. Curiously, no footsteps were echoed in the house because of the soft, noiseless carpeting. However, there was an endless flow of soft music, which the boy would notice later, agreed with the time and temperature of the day.

In his room, Bafemi saw a chess board and a book on chess, his father's present to him for his homecoming. The houseboy withdrew to his quarters. As time passed slowly the boy realised that the house lacked human company. His instinct began to resist the loneliness, in spite of all the material wealth of the house. He switched on the mini-television set in his room. He switched it off an hour later. He reached for his pocket Bible. He opened a psalm. His mind was not attuned. He became restless. The house was an emptiness. There was no mother, neither were there any brothers and sisters. It was a contrast to the beehive of activity at Mama's.

The houseboy called Bafemi for his meal. It was a rich vegetarian meal. He was to learn that his father ate vegetarian meals three times a week. Bafemi wandered round the house, examining each marvel, until he accepted in himself that he was born by a brilliant father. The boy did not analyse the situation. He was not used to self-analysis. He could not do it. Again he went on his knees in his room to pray. His mind felt barren. Slowly sadness closed on him, loneliness descended upon him.

Sulola and Dr Tunji Sotomi came in two hours later. Bafemi, emotionally exhausted, was sleeping across his bed when Sulola and Tunji looked into his room.

'He's asleep,' Sulola said. She looked at the boy fondly, beaming beatifically. They went to the living-room.

'Your son is every inch your replica. I like him. He's big for his age.'

'Thanks. He paints rather well. He carves and sculpts too. I am making a studio for him as his next birthday present. Meanwhile I took all his paintings from his cousin and put them in the guest room.'

'It is not surprising, with a talented father like you. The urge to create runs in the blood.'

They had drinks together.

'Tunji, I think you should call the boy's mother back. From what you have said of her, she is the best woman for you.'

'If there's any woman I want in this house, it is you, Sulola. Business brought us together and I believe in no coincidence, you know. We were brought together to . . . love each other.'

Her liking for him grew each moment she saw him. It was not because of his success. She was successful too, after many struggles that she did not regret. It was because there existed between them an agreeable aura. Whenever they met, their auras were blended harmoniously. Yet she did not want to marry him. She did not want to lose her independence.

'I will never marry, Tunji. Marriage is an interdependent thing. I am not suited for that type of union, nor any other experimental type. I like living in my own place, my own life, not being bothered by the exigencies of marriage. If I was religious I would be a chief priestess. If it were the old days, an empress perhaps.'

There was no air of pride in her. It was her nature she showed. Her being radiated in her sitting position. It reached Tunji.

'If I could marry you, it would be the wedding of the century.'

'You are right. Unfortunately we shall not be wedded. Be strong and courageous enough to give a simple woman a chance. Your wife is simple, too simple and uncomplicated. This is why you do not want her.'

'How do you mean?'

'From what you say of her, she has a simple background, she is pious, uncomplaining, devoted, trusting. You have deceived yourself for years, thinking you are not suited for marriage. After taking me out for a while, you decide overnight that you are again suited for marriage.'

'It's you, Sulola. You always fill me whole.'

She said nothing. Her eyes showed no pride. Her radiance had dignity. Her mind went back to the Odo-Ode project. It was progressing with satisfaction. The new village was changing into the model of a better community. The effect was a boom. All the prosperous sons of the land rushed back bidding to buy land before all the farms were taken. Old Baba refused to sell. This time only the real villagers, those who had always stayed, were to benefit first. As some subtle bribery, the rich children of Odo-Ode donated money for the project. Old Baba accepted the money for the building of the commune, but he did not sell any plot to the sons of the city.

'What's on your mind, Sulola?'

'It's these hawks from the city. They will buy the whole commune if they have the chance; to own a whole village! Over my dead body. We must remain faithful to the old farming families, the artisans. They must keep their land at its priceless value. My uncle is strengthening the family ties. It is the only unit that can work now. The family. From there we become one family again, as it was in the beginning.'

'How?'

'If the family as a unit stood on their portion, and contributed to the Bale, who now represents the commune, it would be better than the networks from the cities. We need an authority which everyone will obey, and it must be the soil itself, the age-old essence of the soil, that appreciates the gift of heaven.'

'You frighten me. Will the old religions come back? All the blood and sacrifice?'

'No. It is a cross between the Islamic and the Christian. You see, the villagers know the codes of love and honesty only through their religion. No village county council will work. When you began this plan, Tunji, it seems you did not consider the spiritual nucleus.'

'Well, the profits will go into the co-operative

ventures on behalf of the people, according to their creeds. I considered an economic nucleus.'

'That's part of it. The villagers themselves want a unit, a ... spiritual unit, the moralising force behind whatever co-operative scheme. This is what my uncle says. That is the way the commune can be healthy, in spite of the buildings and the solar energy.'

Tunji could not bridge his thoughts with hers on that basis. He paced the floor slowly. He remembered the question he asked himself in London. 'What makes a commune work?' The reality of his pet dream was already posing the same question.

'You are right in a way. There must be law and order.'

'Not that type alone. God's laws, as seen through nature, the soil and the harvest. That is what matters in the village. The laws of God reflected in nature, absorbed back to human activities.'

'I am not religious, Sulola, and neither are you, I suppose, but I hate to antagonise you if your plan is backed up by some certainty. Besides, it is only mine to provide the buildings and redevelop the villages. I am a designer, not a priest.'

'That's not all. There must be the presence of God in what you build. I am not religious, I accept. My ways are pagan. I sleep with the men I like, never double-dealing, but that is only because I refuse the codes of marriage.'

'You commit adultery.'

'Yes, but I do not consider the point. I pray to be better in the next incarnation. The city spoilt me. I could have been better in the village. I have no regrets whatsoever. None!'

The music in the room was such that was suitable for the evening, the colour and mood of the atmosphere. Sulola relaxed completely. No one said anything for some time.

Bafemi woke up from his nap, washed and dried his face, and went to the living-room. Sulola's seat faced the entrance door. Tunji had his back to it. Bafemi opened it. Tunji turned and saw his son. His face lit up. Bafemi was strangely impassive.

'Hello, sonny. Can you see him, Sulola? He's growing fast. You've almost caught up with me. How do you like this place?'

Bafemi said nothing because he heard nothing while his gaze caught Sulola's. Hostility flowed from the boy to the woman. Sulola looked away, hurt. Tunji was too much in his joy to notice.

'Don't you like your new place?'

'It is like a house in the films ... I have never seen a place like it.'

'Do you like it?'

He shrugged his shoulders. 'I don't know.'

Tunji's brow was furrowed. It was then he saw the disapproval on his son's face. He said nothing.

'Tunji introduce me to your son.'

'Oh, this is my son Bafemi and Bafemi, this is Auntie Sulola.'

Bafemi remained cold. The other two felt uneasy. Sulola got up to go.

'Yes, Sulola, I'll take you home.'

Bafemi said an ineffective goodbye. He went back to his room, still angrier. This was not the life he wanted. He abhored this homestead.!

Outside, in the car, Sulola sighed.

'That's a tough male you have. He does not approve of me. But I like him very much. That boy is on his mother's side. You've got trouble coming if you continue to run after me and the other girls.'

'He'll grow out of it. By the way, I have not seen Mope since that tour.' He did not mention the pregnancy.

'Well, good for you. We shall have to leave each other sooner or later, Tunji. Call back your wife. Call back Mary.'

'Suppose she intends to get married to someone else? We have to think of that.'

'Yes, but try first. Try first and see how she reacts to it.'

Mope was two months pregnant. She wore her best trendy dress and called a taxi for the E.C.E. She obeyed Baba Ake's instructions to the letter. She should see Tunji only when the pregnancy was two months old. Mope was confident. She paid off the taxi and went up the elevator.

Tunji's secretary said: 'Dr Sotomi will not receive visitors without appointments. Would you like to book an appointment please?'

'No. I want to see him right now.' Mope's chewing-gum smacked noisily.

'I am afraid you cannot see him. He is busy at the moment.'

'Why don't you ask him first, before you start giving me that crap!'

The secretary glowered at Mope. She restrained herself. It was part of the etiquette of her profession and never had she worked in a place that so much respected order and etiquette. 'Here work is work, no messing.' That was Tunji's occasional phrase to any slack staff. The secretary pressed the intercom.

'There is a young lady here, wanting to see you, sir. She insists on seeing you without an appointment.'

'Em . . . What's her name?'

Mope leaned over the intercom, and snarled, 'It's me – Mope!'

'Let her in.' Mope was allowed to enter. The secretary closed the door after her. She said under her breath, 'I wonder what he's got with her!'

Mope sat on the easy chair, threw back her head. Tunji stared at her, drumming his fingers on the desk. The chewing gum smacked and hissed between the teeth and tongue.

'I want to move in, to your place. A woman who's expecting a baby should have a man to protect her.'

'You cannot move in to my place because I don't want you there. You have the child and I'll take it. I'll see the Welfare about you.'

'You are not chucking me out like that! You are so stuffed up with your own pride. I am going to live in your house. I'm carrying our child. Not just mine, ours! Tell the Welfare what? I won't be treated with shame. You hear that? You had me over and over again and you're not going to chuck me out now like a piece of rag. And so you want to make me a child-producing machine? Rubbish? I am moving into your house!'

'Will you stop shouting! You have to realise that I have no feeling for you.'

'Are you not ashamed of that? What are you, a dog sticking his hind to every bitch? You will take me and the child in.'

For a moment, Tunji was confused and angry, not only with Mope, but with himself. What had made him take up with such an uncouth woman?

'You are so uncouth, Mope. I don't know why I let you touch my skin.'

Waving her hands wildly in the air, she raged, 'Who do you think you are? I do not care if all the world pays you homage. I have known many men, yet it is not a man who refuses his responsibility. Apart from your rotten pendulum, you are not a man! Are you a man? Are you a man at all?'

He stood up from the desk and took quick strides to her. He slapped her, knocking her to the floor. He went to the window, brought out a cigarette and smoked silently. She had not expected the slap. She did not believe he could slap a woman, because of his fine manners. When he hit her, her head was rattled by the shock. She panted on the floor. The chewing gum fell out of her mouth.

'Beast! Beast, beast, beast . . . You beast of no gender!' She was now crying hysterically. It lasted for almost an hour. At last she stopped, realising that he would not comfort her. Slowly she wiped her face and her sniffs died down.

'Are you sober now?' he asked.

She did not say anything.

'It's good that you are.'

'Please, Tunji, take me into the house.' It was her new tactic. 'Is it not shameful to keep me outside? It is your child, Tunji, a child like your other children.'

His heart softened. He smoked, eyeing her intensely. 'I can get a flat for you. A good flat for you and the child.'

'Does the child not have your own blood? Is he damned because it is the result of our own union? It is not a slave child I bear, Tunji … It is your child.'

'All right, all right!' The spell struck him and in spite of himself, he yielded. It worked because it was his own selfish indulgence, gathering the dust of repercussions.

'Yes, but only for the sake of the baby. You can come in. I'll send a driver to collect your things. You will stay in a separate room. Now go, and let me have some peace, if you please.'

Mope went out with a flippant carriage. Tunji went out later in search of Sulola. He found her on a building site, her current building contract. She was directing the labourers in the hot sun. When she saw Tunji's Range Rover grind to a stop, she went over to him. He asked her if he could see her. She promised to see him at a restaurant when she finished work. He drove off. He did not go back to the office. He just drove on, making a subconscious circuit of this vast tropical city. After a while he parked the car and began to think.

It was inconceivable for him to lose his grip on his affairs. Everything had to be securely held in his control. This mattered to him as a man. He always planned and got what he wanted. Mope was proving a problem. On what grounds could he, the confident Dr Sotomi, make sure that Mope existed in the house without any contact between them? Her presence in the house would be frustrating. It also meant meeting Sulola outside if he wanted to prevent unpleasant scenes between the two women in front of Bafemi. He asked himself if he had lost the control he had in England, the confidence to decide without changing the decision if it was harmless to his well-being. He was amazed that he could not bring within bounds the unruly temperament of Mope, and that he had failed to sense it, as he had always done in his associations with people. Tunji's every wave of dissent must lose its ebb. This female creature he would tame. He started the car and drove back in time for the rendezvous with Sulola.

He told her that the first phase of the commune would be completed the following year. There were a few machines to be imported for the solar unit.

She noticed his changed expression and asked, 'What is troubling you, Tunji?'

'That bitch Mope.' He told her the story from its beginning to its present unpleasant chapter.

'You men are all the same. What made you think that she was just a receiving vessel? These young girls are more vicious than their mothers. There are more feminists around today than ever before. In her own way she is one of them.'

'Is that all you can say, Sulola?'

'No, darling. I do not like the girl. I always remember that panther look she gave me. I can only say this, if you feel nothing for her, make sure that she does not ruin you. Some of them do; they simply make their husbands mad.'

'I will not run mad because of that one. I shall refuse to know her further, after she gives birth. I shall starve her of myself physically and emotionally until she packs up and goes. But I'll keep the child. You see, Sulola, she seems to have trapped me. I feel it every time I think of it and this is why I will make sure that she is caught in her own web.'

'It looks very much like a trap.' She gave him a life-filling smile. His mind relaxed. His plan looked feasible to him. He realised that he needed Sulola more than he had ever realised.

'Sulola, why don't we . . . let's get married?'

'Why do you waste your time on such speculations?' Her eyes were lost suddenly in sadness. Then slowly she said: 'I did not tell you one thing. It was hard for me to have my late sons. After them the doctor said I could have no more. The native doctors said the same. You see, Tunji, in my quest for children, I took so much from men, that I'd prefer to live the rest of my life single than ever marry. I know that what I feel for you, I have never felt before. Each time I give you my body, our minds seem to hold an infinite dialogue. I have never felt like that towards any other man.'

'I am sorry,' he said to her. She was very sad.

'I love children. The ones I had died, and I cannot have any more, ever. You see, I believe that I should not sink into despair. I believe I should absorb this misfortune and hope for the best in my next incarnation as my village teaches. So I decided to struggle with men until I got to where I am.'

'You don't look your age, though. You look younger. You have taken it well.'

'That is as it should be, Tunji.'

They met again in the evening. Their appearance in the night clubs attracted the attention of the band leaders. Always, some impromptu compositions were made in their names, as was the greedy custom of the minstrels. They sang people's praises for money. In the case of these two elite customers, it spread the news of their association in town and abroad. It did not encourage Mary in the north. It made Bafemi more and more bitter against his father.

Mope was now huge with child. It disgusted Bafemi. When the young woman moved in, he received her with nonchalance. They did not eat at the table at the same time. He gave her only the usual greeting in the morning, afternoon and evening. They were complete strangers. It did not help either of the two in any emotional way. The boy could not reconcile his father's age with Mope's. To him she was no older than any of his immediate older cousins. Therefore, he found no basis for respecting Mope. She decided that Bafemi was a 'devil', if he could stay in the house without any warmth towards her.

Her worst experience came from Tunji's behaviour. He did not stay at home often and when he did, it was to be with his son. What Mope did not realise was that for

Tunji, she did not exist. All he waited for was the delivery of the child. She also did not realise that every time the man went into his son's room, it was to try and win the boy over. Every time he tried, he found a firm resistance.

Bafemi's studies deteriorated. He did not read any more, because he could not concentrate. He did not go to his art lessons. He did not go to Woli. A claustrophobic air enclosed him completely, so much so that when the entrance examinations to the college came, he failed every paper woefully.

Deji gained admission to the Government Academy. Bafemi temporarily lost touch with his childhood friends. Tunji Sotomi's concern grew and one day it exploded into anger. It was in his office. Sulola was present.

'It is scandalous! It is as if you are not my own son. I have given you everything that you need. You hardly seem to respect me. Now you have failed all your exams! I am not going round to beg the school principals to take you in. You will repeat!'

Sulola moved over to Bafemi and made as if to hold him. He avoided her. She was hurt.

Tunji became mad with anger. He fumed: 'You are so insolent. Heaven knows what kind of training my sister gave you. Now go home by taxi. The car won't take you home. I am cutting your pocket money by half. I will remove the T.V. set from your room and I will think of other things to discipline you. Go home!'

Bafemi went out of the room, unmoved. He remembered clearly what had happened at school.

'Big-goggles' their class teacher sat behind the desk munching *guguru* and groundnut. It was breaktime. Big-goggles was looking through the list of the new entrants to the secondary schools. His eyes peered at the list with a weak albino focus. In class, Big-goggles' crunch-crunch whetted the appetite of hungry pupils. He hardly had his mouth still. It was always crunch, crunch-crack, crunch, crack-crack, crunch. This was how he earned his name 'Big-goggles the guguru-eater'.

The bell for the end of break went. Big-goggles looked up and quiet settled in the class, except for the crunch-crunch of his mouth. His Adam's apple slid up and down. He cleared his throat, ran his tongue over his teeth, deep into the corners of the mouth, sucking the guguru that was stuck. He brought out a blue handkerchief on which an amateur hand had embroidered 'Goodnight Darling. Sleep well my angel'. As usual Big-goggles held out the handkerchief. A ludicrous shadow crossed his face and disappeared almost immediately. He meticulously removed his glasses, and cleared them. The Adam's apple rose and fell.

The ritual was over. The class could begin.

'Yes, I have been going through the list of successful entrants. Some of you are seeds that have fallen by the wayside. After months of coaching, it is shocking to see some of you failing. Next year some pupils will be wearing sparkling white uniforms with canvas shoes to match, while others will still be in the brown uniform of primary schools.'

He was walking round the class. Soon he had reached Bafemi's row. He turned to the boy. 'Bafemi Sotomi, you are a disgrace to your family. Stand up and let the class see you.'

Bafemi stood up, assailed by the 'boos' of the class.

'All of you look at that boy well. You all know that he has the brains, but does he want to work?'

The whole class chorused: 'No-oo!'

'Perhaps he has his eyes on his father's wealth. Listen everybody, ardent regrets await the unwise pupil. There will be sobs in future for the truant.'

The boy had then bowed his head in humiliation. He did not cry.

Now, waiting for the taxi, he decided to go to Bayo Cole's studio. The door of the studio opened to him. Bayo's eyes lit up in amazement. He had not seen Bafemi for a long time. All the suppressed emotions of the boy erupted and spilled over in complaints. Bayo let him talk. He hoped that would ease the boy. Gradually the storm ebbed.

'I hate him, Cousin Bayo. I hate all of them. Sulola, his Madam, is driving him crazy. That other one Mope is a sloppy one. They all seem so vulgar that I cannot live there any longer. Help me, Cousin Bayo. Let me stay with you!'

He looked at the artist. his eyes bold with pleading.

'As you know this is not like your father's house. We'll have to do the cooking together. Sometimes you'll go to the market after school, before you have your lessons. There will be no house servants.'

'I don't care, Cousin Bayo. As long as you let me live with you.'

'Why not Mama?'

'She will send me back to my father. Let me stay, please.'

'All right, we'll go and see your father this evening.'

The artist took his apprentice to Tunji Sotomi. Tunji agreed without any hesitation, asking Bayo to discipline Bafemi well. It was Tunji's opinion that the material comfort of the house had spoilt his son.

'You know I am a busy man, but he will have to make a success out of his own life.'

Bafemi's things were packed. He left the wonder-house that evening. For the first time in months a flicker of joy lit up in him.

The following year was an emergence from the shadows into bright light for the boy. Bafemi threw his whole force into his studies. This time he was determined to pass his exams.

His creative pastime so much pleased Bayo that the artist himself felt that soon, the apprentice would be master. Bafemi loved the beauty of colours, the magic of light and shadows in paintings. He expressed himself with passion, reacting to a strong creative impulse. In art he took refuge and rejoiced.

His contact with Woli was renewed and the Adept continued to implant knowledge in the child: knowledge that tended to make an adult out of the child.

The exams came. Bafemi passed and entered the Government Academy. Then he returned to his father's house, from where he went into the school boarding house.

The wonder-house still remained brimful of the drama of Mope and Sulola.

Eight

When Bafemi left for his cousin's Mope was left alone in the house. The ripeness of her pregnancy brought its fatigue and the need for comfort. Tunji was never in the house to comfort her. Mope bore the child in her womb with the pain that comes with any unwanted burden. Often she sat thinking, wondering if it was worthwhile to have a child for him. Baba Ake's advice, that she should be patient till she gave birth, kept her going. She hoped that a strong system would be used to make Tunji stay at home.

Now heavy with child, and with its birth imminent, she stood before her long dressing mirror. She observed how pathetically her eyes stared back at her. It was then she had the cold feeling of nausea. She began to sweat, a very cold sweat. She made for her bed, feeling dizzy. She sat down under the weight of imminent motherhood. The faintness became intense. She could hardly focus. She supported herself with her hands, her protrusion bulging before her. Her face felt sweaty. She wanted to call for help, but her lips became tight shut in spite of herself. The new life in her demanded a complete physical surrender from her. She struggled for strength. Paradoxically, the more she tried, the more the necessity of maternity made her feel exhausted. She began to cry, as a violent sensation rose from her fertile depths and her thighs became flushed by seminal fluids.

The houseboy was not in. The house had its constant vibration of gentle music.

Mope's eyes closed. Her mouth was parted by a deep groan as another vicious contraction rose from deep within. Another rush of warm slimy liquid flushed her thighs.

She fell flat on her back, onto the bed. A shadow crept into her. As she opened her mouth, she could hear her own shrill cry. It stabbed the air, tearing away on self-multiplying octaves. She lost consciousness.

The scream reached the houseboy who was coming back from his daily shopping. Providence had it that he took the front door this time, instead of the back door. The houseboy then took charge. He knew what to do, because he had once helped an elder sister.

He dashed to Mope's room. He took her legs and put them gently on to the bed, straightening the upper part of her body. He spread her legs wide apart, propped her head with a pillow.

He dived next for the telephone and got Tunji's office.

'Massa, massa, na madam ... make you come quick!'

'Which madam? Sulola? Tell her to come to the office.'

'No. Na yer wife. De one wey get belle. I think say de time don reach for de pickin. Make you come quick.'

'Right.' Tunji told the office telephonist to get his doctor. He left a message for him. Without waiting a second, he got into his car and made for home. The doctor arrived at the same time. Together they went into the house.

The doctor gave her one look and said, 'Delivery is due in the next few hours. I'll call for my clinic's ambulance and we'll take care of her there. She will be all right. Its not unusual for this to happen.'

The air of urgency died down when Mope was taken to the clinic of the family doctor.

Helping and gentle hands rested expertly on her stomach. Her final efforts began. Tears rolled down her cheeks. The kind eyes of medical experts looked towards her with reassurance. The pangs increased. The midwife let Mope hold her wrist. The throes of childbirth started her yelling. Everything was focused on the birth. The rest of existence ceased for her at that moment. Her mind and body were a concentrated point of the pain which every mother must know, and which each could bear according to her strength.

The doctor had his hands in sterilised gloves like the

rest of the staff. They waited, ready between her thighs. The head of the new arrival appeared as fine blood flowed through. An infantile cry was heard when the new arrival experienced the first rush of air into its lungs. The lungs took in the breath of life. The mother lay panting, completely exhausted.

It was a bouncing baby boy.

Seyidi, the Doctor with the capital D, always parked his car alongside the kerb in front of Mary's house. This was the young psychiatrist who would not erase the face of Mary from his mind. At first, he refused to react to the impulse for the sake of professional etiquette. Six months later he made his first courageous visit to Mary. He had not stopped going since then, for one reason. He was still trying to convince the woman to forget her past marriage and accept another man into her life.

'Seyidi, I like you, but I cannot marry you because I do not think my feeling is strong enough for marriage. There are younger women who obviously like you. I am older than you, am I not?'

'That does not matter.'

'Agreed, but my children may not take kindly to a second marriage. I would hate to hurt them, because I love them very much.'

'What makes you think they won't like it?'

'I know they won't like it. You see, Seyidi, should I, because I insist on a certain ephemeral happiness, tell my children that they have to readjust, no matter what? I believe that would be selfish. Don't you?'

'You are deep. This is why I like you. I disregard, of course, the circumstance of our meeting.'

'I disregard that phase of my life too in so far as I am sure I do not admire you because you were the glamorous doctor who gave me life. I like you because you deserve my respect. Simply I believe God helped you to give me back my sanity.'

Seyidi kept going to Mary's home. Her father liked him. Her mother regarded him as a son. He had many moments with the family. It was not unexpected, sooner or later, for Mary's father to start pleading on his behalf. Mary refused his hand in marriage. They went out together very often but as platonic companions.

He found her too adamant to convince. After a while, he became patient and waited for the eventual consent.

'I will not marry anyone else. It would be disastrous however if we both grow old, me as a bachelor and you as a divorcee,' Seyidi said.

'I'll still have my children. What about you?'

'Don't try to discourage me, Mary. If you have your children, and I love you for ever, I will love your children as if I were their father.'

Such were the occasional dialogues between Mary and the Doctor. They kept on seeing each other. When Bafemi gained admission into the secondary school, they sent him a joint present and celebrated the event with a night out.

The boy took Seyidi for a genuine 'uncle'. He believed that he did not know most of his mother's family relations. And so he replied to his 'uncle's' letters whenever they came. The letters were very casual, and they suggested nothing that would betray Seyidi's intentions. Tunji Sotomi did not know of 'Uncle Seyidi'. Bafemi simply did not communicate very much with his father, in those days.

From her old lonely ways, Mary's life was blossoming. She had many friends in the church. She helped many church societies and won the affection of several old women and children. Her daughter, Ayodele was attending a junior primary school and she was every inch her mother. Often Ayodele asked her mother if she could go to the south and stay with her father, Tunji Sotomi. Mary assured her daughter that the time had not come for such a move.

One evening Mary's father called her. The man was now growing old. Mary observed his greying crop of hair. He was going to retire from the railways in a year's time. He cleared his throat, and gave his daughter one of his amiable smiles.

'Mary, it is about Seyidi and Tunji. I have tried to

persuade you many times on the subject, and I will not push it further, but ... Mary, Seyidi deserves an answer, a definite one, within the next six months. That is the first thing. Two, it is not my wish that you should be a half-married woman. What is the use of pretending you are still Mrs Sotomi when obviously you are not? Grant Tunji his divorce. Again within the next six months. Then we shall all know where you stand.'

'Father, I cannot marry Seyidi.'

'Why not?'

'My children.'

'So they will be the first whose mother is taking a second husband!' The old man laughed with sarcasm. 'It is for their sake you should marry again, while they are young. Mary, you are not living a complete life. The complete life that our fathers recommend. A woman should not make herself the man and the wife. That is what you are doing. You want us to believe you can do without a man. All right, you have tried, very well ... but we can see that for a woman like you, there should be a man.'

'I love Tunji, Father.'

'After so many years! This is ridiculous! When did you last live together as husband and wife? Mary, don't deceive yourself. Face reality.'

'The reality is that the only man I can give myself to is Tunji.'

'Now, in what class is your son?'

'Form Two, going on very soon to three.'

'So he must be in his middle teens. All I am saying is that if he does not understand now, he will accept it later.'

'Father, he is not here to state his own case.'

'There is no case to state. Is he not just a boy?'

'No, Father, the children of today are not like those of yesterday. They ask the whys and the hows. For their sake I will remain as I am. As for the divorce, I will grant Tunji all he asks for. I will give him no hindrance. But instead of six months, I'll ask for a year. Perhaps he may still change his mind. You see, in every letter Bafemi writes, he begs me to be patient. He seems to have hopes like me.'

'Like mother, like son; hoping for miracles! Fair enough. But accept my own proposition too. A year is long enough for you to change your mind and marry Seyidi, yes?'

She regarded the palms of her hands and smiled vaguely. 'Why not? That's fair enough. He should take whatever answer I give.'

Her father declared the conversation closed. He hoped that Mary would change her mind. It was not his wish to see his own daughter grow old as a divorcee. She was still young enough for a second marriage, to his way of thinking.

Mope left her one-year-old son at home with the housemaid. She hurried through the alleys, shortening her long trek, throwing glances over her shoulders. She was making sure that no acquaintance could see her. She clasped her handbag firmly to herself, under her armpit.

Baba Ake was just finishing with a client. He smiled on seeing Mope. She greeted him in a sullen voice. The departing client had hardly stepped into the alleyway before Mope started:

'Baba, that man is a devil. You have to do something. My child is now a year old. I weaned him off the breast nine months ago. My man does not even look at me, much less come to my bed. I cannot stay in the house as if I was a ghost. He does not treat me like someone who has any life to be considered. Do something, Baba! He sleeps outside with his whore since his son entered the secondary school and he always tells me that when I have had enough, I can pack and go. I want to stay. I am getting nowhere!'

Baba Ake took her excitement calmly. He was used to all sorts of clients. There were those who had the profound coolness to make their consultation. There were those who were so desperate, that it required skill and practice to get the facts out of them.

'I will give you one thing. You will hang it over the fireplace in the kitchen, covered in soot. As you cook, and the heat of the fire radiates to the amulet, his passion for you will leap like flames.'

'We have no such fireplace.'

'What, don't you eat in your house?'

'His kitchen is modern. There is no soot there. It is clean. Too clean for any amulet to be hidden over any fireplace.'

Baba Ake laughed. 'Not to worry, child. There is another type. You will put that in his meal, well prepared with fish . . .'

'I don't cook his food.'

'Who does? Are you not his wife?'

'He does not treat me like one. A houseboy cooks his meals. And there is no hope of winning the boy over. He is a stupid lout. He might tell his master.'

Baba Ake leaned back, scratched his head, dug in his pouch for a kola-nut and chewed in silence. Then he smiled and asked: 'Tell me, how did you get yourself involved with this type of man . . . ?'

She shrugged her shoulders.

Baba Ake smiled again with confidence.

'There is a very powerful thing we can do. I'll keep a fireplace burning for you with a charm hanging over it. Then you will take another one home and put it under his pillow. Sew it in, if you can. It will work. There is nothing like it. He will do your bidding. Next time you come here, I am sure it will be to thank me. The fees are high. Eighty Naira.'

'I have twenty Naira on me now. I'll bring the remaining money tomorrow.'

'All right, I trust you as a good client.'

She left, feeling very pleased with herself.

When the houseboy was out, it was easy for Mope to enter Tunji's room and stay long enough to sew the amulet into the interior of the pillow-case. She used a safety pin to tack it down for extra security. She turned the patched side down. She was determined to remember to remove the pillow-case before it was due for laundry.

Then, she went into the living-room, poured herself a drink, and awaited her victory. Late at night, Tunji came in. He saw her in the living-room and said a casual greeting.

'And here comes the demi-god. Tunji, do you think what you are doing is fair?'

'You have no claim on me, Mope. You used the child as a pretext. Now you have it. Sooner or later you will leave. I won't push you, but you will simply pack and go. I will then see the Welfare about you.'

'We shall see. That prostitute you sleep with outside has bewitched you. One day her spell will break and we shall see.'

She left the room. He swore under his breath. 'What a life!'

He took a shower, shaved and read the newspapers. Later he went to bed. He sank into the circular bed, blacked out the room with a bed switch, put on a soft orange light and listened to a late night programme on his quadrophonic set. It was a warm evening. He completely stripped, enjoying the sensuality of nudity. He pressed one switch. An evening breeze came into the room with the natural chill of nature. He got into his sheets.

'I have told this boy never to stuff my pillows up like this!'

He turned the pillows over, put two on the side, then sank back into bed. A sharp end pierced his scalp. He jumped out of bed, switched on the lights. He felt some wetness on his scalp. He moved his fingers there and touched blood. He saw it. He became more puzzled. He took the pillow, examined it. He saw the fine tacks of white cotton. He traced them to a safety-pin which was unhooked, its sharp end dangerously protruding. Tunji carefully put his hand into the pillow-case, and made to bring out the pin. It felt heavy. He then removed the pillow completely, out of the case. He turned the inside of the case out. Glaring at him was the amulet.

In flitting seconds, the whole issue dawned on him.

He threw the pillow-case back on the bed.

'Dirty bitch! . . . ' he sneered under his breath. He put on his pyjamas, and then his dressing-gown. He strode out of his room.

He kicked open the door of her room. The child started to cry. Mope's eyes popped out of her head, as she struggled to understand the transition between sleep and wakefulness. He pulled her violently across the bed and let her fall on the floor. Her cloth came off her body. She was naked. She groped for her wrap and tied it round herself in feverish movements. He dealt her two sharp blows across the face. Her eyes saw lights of various colours. She fell back on the bed.

The baby was crying. The noise of his mother's tears covered his completely. Tunji watched her. He lit himself a cigarette slowly.

'You are the only woman I have ever slapped and I do not mind lashing you all over again. Go and pick up the amulet in my room.'

She cowered on the bed.

'I said, go and pick it up, you bitch.' She ran out of the room, losing her sense of pride completely.

He followed her into his room.

'Pick that damned thing up!'

She picked it up.

'You put it there, did you not? Answer me! Did you put it there?'

'Yes,' she said slowly. The humiliation she felt could never be worse.

'You are finished. You planned it so well. Planned it so well that your black magic became your god. You are finished! How do you think I would marry a creature like you? Now take that thing into the kitchen and burn it. I want to see you dispose of the ash, pillow-case and all.'

She trembled all over. She looked at him, a thousand pleas for mercy in her eyes. 'I am afraid, Tunji. I cannot burn it.'

'You cannot what . . .? Pick up the bloody thing. What made you dabble in things you could not touch?

Bitchy devil! I will drive you into the open air if you don't burn that thing.'

Silently, she took the pillow-case and the amulet. He threw a box of matches at her. She picked it up. She went towards the kitchen. Tunji followed her. She burned the amulet and the pillow-case. The smoke had the odour of burning leather. The polluted air was sucked away by the kitchen's cyclic ventilation system. The ash went down the waste chute.

'Mope, this is your last night under my roof. You will pack up your things and get out tomorrow or I'll call the police to do it for you. You have never been my wife. As for the child, I will pay into the Welfare Board for its upkeep. When he is old enough I'll bring him to live with me.'

He left her and went back to bed. Mope sat on a stool in her bedroom, feeling the world close in on her. She hated herself at that moment. Her son stopped crying, but he lay awake, sharing the sleeplessness of his mother.

Another phase began in Mope's life. She was forced to leave the following day. Tunji gave her some money to resettle her. She stayed with a friend for a few days. Then she took a room in downtown Ibadan – the cheapest she could afford. This new phase of her life demanded extreme frugality from her. She could not afford the luxuries of frequent taxi rides, neither could she enjoy the past pleasures of rich cuisine. She sold some of her clothes to pay for the furniture she needed immediately. Now she had no job, since she had turned herself into a housewife when she moved into Tunji's house. Also, Tunji only gave her enough for her son's upkeep. She always looked forward to the monthly remittance. Each week, each month, added to her remorse. Already the marks of hard life began to show. The plump flesh was drained off her body by the sweat of a more demanding life.

When she saw Baba Ake next, the old man refused to accept the blame. He saw her story written in her own face. Callously he asked for his fees.

'Look, daughter, I did my own part of the bargain. It

must be your own fault. Perhaps nature does not want you to be with this man. That is your destiny, not mine. I did my job very well. If you used my juju well, that man would have been yours.'

'Baba, I have no money.'

'*Oga ta, oga o ta, owo alaru a pe,*' the old man retorted. It was his to do his job. It was his to receive his fees. It was not his to pay the price of risks.

'Baba, I cannot pay you the remaining sixty ₦aira.'

'I accept a monthly payment. Do you think I live on sand? What do you people think? Medicine is no plaything. You don't joke with spirits. I deal only in justice. If it is not right for you, re-examine yourself. Come every month to pay me twenty ₦aira, until you pay the whole debt.'

Mope pleaded endlessly. Baba Ake lived up to his ruthless reputation. In the end, he agreed to a six-monthly repayment. She went home reliving her past years in regrets. The city opened itself to several ways of earning money. Gradually she was led by other friends, with whom she shared similar frustrations and neuroses, into escapades. These escapades included nights out with men who wanted to pay for their illicit pleasures. With this extra money in hand, she hoped to make a comeback to life. Her road through life would be lined by men of many shades of character, all looking for pleasure, for which they paid high prices, and which also drained her gradually of her flesh.

Bafemi had become the pride of the art master as soon as he entered the Government Academy. He proved himself a good student. Those who knew him intimately, like Deji, noticed the reserve in him. Bafemi was a swot because books offered an escape from his miseries. Art also served as a pleasurable refuge. He suppressed the thoughts of his father's domestic life, but when they came, he ardently wished that his father would summon back his mother, now that Mope was gone.

To the boy's chagrin, his father showed no sign of any

such design. Instead, Tunji Sotomi began to press Sulola for marriage. It became clearer to Bafemi that his father's home offered no happiness, in spite of its material splendour. This was why he never looked forward to the vacations.

Deji, Bafemi's friend, was then in the fourth form. Somehow he felt that he knew what would give Bafemi some vivacity of life. In the school, from the third form onwards, the imported subculture of music and drugs provided what only the adventurer could enjoy. The 'scene' as it was called began on Saturday and went on till Sunday, at a place called 'Jordan'. Deji often persuaded Bafemi to join in the 'day-tripping' because it was the only experience that knew no horizons in its infinite pleasures.

'Why don't you come along this weekend, ehn? You'll like it. Girls, music, you know. There are three fan letters for you too. You were so good at the school's last arts festival. You dig?'

'No, Deji.'

'Will you kill yourself because of your father? Rubbish, man, rubbish. He's got his own life and you've got your own thing man. And your own thing is sweet when you're young. All those dames falling for you and you refuse? I ain't seen no one throw away his own honey, man. You got to lick it, cause it's yours.'

'Where is the party?'

'Jordan. You don't know it. But I'll take you there. Heavy sound and all. Stereo, man, stereo!'

Deji was utterly irresistible at that moment. Bafemi yielded to his persuasions.

'Look, Bafemi, boys must be boys. See?' Deji laughed. 'Ooo, when a man is young, he's got to bang life and bang it solid. Right? Oh sure thing. All this mama-papa unhappiness will go, you know. Okay?'

Bafemi nodded. Deji added: 'Right on, brother.'

Jordan was a bamboo shelter, built right outside the boundary of the school compound. It belonged to the Agricultural Development Board and was only used during the maize harvest seasons. The students bribed the watchman often and equipped the place with a stereo sound set. The music kept the party going. Attendance was exclusive to a small unit of boys and girls, between the ages of fifteen and nineteen.

Once upon a time someone called it Jordan, because of the river that flowed in the environs. The bamboo room became Jordan.

The party was on when Deji and Bafemi reached Jordan at ten that Saturday evening. It was an intimate unit of boys and girls, moving, dancing, laughing, hugging, moaning in clouds of smoke that floated under the red glow of the electric light. The stereophonic music had the cadences of whines, booms and other sonic systems.

The vibrant centre of Jordan Bamboo had musical pulsations that captured the raw and inexperienced emotions of the boy. In awe and uncertainty, Bafemi joined this group of youth. He wondered if the place was safe from official intrusion. He looked towards Deji, who was rolling himself what he called a 'joint.' Bafemi's eyes caught a girl's. She was a slim thing in skin-tight jeans, topless blouse, with a bronze African pendant dropping between the mounds of her breasts.

She smiled lazily at him, leaning against a bamboo post, smoking. Her movements were slow and indolent. Bafemi looked away. His eyes caught a trio, sitting on the floor. They were two boys and a girl. The girl sat in the middle giggling. The boys laughed too. Then she stopped, protruded her tongue, sharply. She turned to the one on the right. He brought out his tongue too. They brought their tongues together, their eyes looking straight at each other. The touch of the tongues was quick and gentle. She turned to the boy on her left and the same ritual was performed. Then the trio laughed. Bafemi looked away.

'Here, have a drag,' Deji said. 'Come on, don't be a square. Have a drag. Try it, mate, there's nothing like it. Come on …!'

Bafemi accepted the roll of marijuana.

'Like I did it. Suck it in, hold it in and release it …

gently. That's it. Have another one ... Superb.'

Bafemi handed it over. Deji laughed, patting him on the back. The two boys laughed together.

Bafemi leaned against a bamboo. The floor felt lighter under his feet. He grinned.

'You are happy, you know,' Deji said. 'Very happy. Life is sweet, man, really sweet.'

Bafemi continued grinning. The topless girl moved towards Bafemi, also grinning. She pressed him to the bamboo frame with her full body, voluptuously. She continued to smile, looking into his eyes. No one paid any attention to them. The music syncopated to a slow rocking beat. The topless girl rocked slowly from side to side grinding herself to him, flesh to flesh.

'I wrote two letters to you,' she said. 'I like your paintings at the regional arts festival. Mmm, I admire you. I could do a nude for you. I don't mind.'

She grinned. He grinned too. She rocked him slowly, now moving him with herself.

'My name is Althea. Grew up in England ... Mmm I like you. Will you dip your feeler into my nectar, for a loving pollination? ... I dig you ... so much ... Mmm.'

She moved up her lips to his and they merged with magnetic energy.

Animal passions rise easily, more easily perhaps, than the rich and sublime emotions of the artist.

Bafemi was a virgin. The storm that came within had the ferocity of tumbling fresh waterfalls. Althea rested her head on his chest and she rocked him still to the rhythm of the music. How long they remained so, he could not tell. However, the lights went out at midnight. It was the tradition of the youth then to know each other through physical intimacy.

A fake gospel of love ruled their passions. They threw centuries of traditional inhibitions overboard and celebrated nature, as they conceived it, in their nakedness. It was, they believed, to make 'love' and not war. To every boy, a girl yielded herself and for some it was an orgy of multiple experiences.

Althea led Bafemi away in the darkness and made

him sink into the long evening grass. Her tenderness stunned him. The foundation of his moral formation began to crack. In vain he tried to recall his senses, but his flesh was aflame with lust and it was too hard for him to halt his new emotion.

Afterwards he rolled over to her side, sensing her sweat. She believed it was the ultimate fulfilment of love as it was meant to be from the time of Adam and Eve. She believed that it was as it should be, according to the new gospels of imported subculture. And so she felt grateful to him. She could not then see his eyes, brimful as they were with visions of self-pity. He felt sick inside. When she heard him moan, she took it for ecstatic release and so she thanked him the more.

'You make me feel like a real woman,' she said.

He did not understand her because he was overwhelmed by a deep remorse.

Nine

Sulola knocked and entered Bafemi's room.

'Bafemi, I've come to greet you and to congratulate you on your success in the terminal exams.'

Bafemi did not say anything. He only looked away, once, from his game of solitaire. The chess board was in front of him.

'Thank you.' His eyes found the ceiling.

'Bafemi, come,' she added. 'Please come.'

Her plea amazed him. He looked quizzically at her and then he rose and walked slowly to her.

'I am inviting you and your father for lunch at my place. This will be the umpteenth time that I have invited you. Will you come this time?'

Bafemi said nothing.

'Come.' They both sat on the two chairs in the room. 'I knew you when you were younger and I have loved you since then like my own child. But you are always against me. I know it has to do with your mother. You are not a child, Bafemi, and you have heard me argue consistently with your father. I have nothing against your mother's return. I desire it. I am not going to be your father's next wife. I am going away, for new duties in my village.'

Bafemi was not convinced of her sincerity. She read his mind on his face because he continued to frown. She reached for his hands with fondness. He gently withdrew them. She could not find her own words. With trembling hands she brought out an envelope.

'Take this, Bafemi. This is your first-class return train ticket to Jos. Perhaps a trip to your mother will change things for the better. Now is another chance.'

He took the envelope from her and said a faint 'thank you'. She went out of the room, closing the door softly behind her. She lit a fresh cigarette, joining Tunji in the living-room.

'Sulola, you are wasting your time.'

'As soon as they finish the second phase of construction of the new Odo-Ode, I will leave, Tunji, and nothing will stop me.'

'You will marry me, woman. It's you or no one else.'

The train jerked forward to begin its overnight journey to Jos. While his father waved once, Sulola kept waving till the train took its first bend. When Tunji and his woman friend were lost to view, Bafemi began to think about Sulola. He could not determine her character other than that of a society woman, whom some would refer to as a free D-madam, or more vulgarly as *asewo*, which simply meant prostitute.

The train moved through the night with the monotonous sound of the locomotive. Bafemi slept in the comfortable first-class car. He woke at dawn to see that they had reached Jebba. He opened the window and let in the humid air of dawn. Fish-sellers scurried down the platform.

Soon the locomotive resumed its journey, swaying from side to side in a rhythmic regularity. Daylight became clearer and revealed the vegetation of savannah. In the early slant of the sun it was becoming hot. The boy took his copy of *Reader's Digest* and began to read. He dozed off.

Lunch hour came and went. Thoughts of Althea came to him and he resisted the spirit of the night they had spent together. As he referred to it, it was the night of flesh and sin. He did not relish any repetition of it. Any time the thought of Althea came, he chased it away with a mighty effort.

Althea was not easily forgotten. She was determined not to let Bafemi forget her. The week following their experience, she wrote a long letter to him; it was a mixed espistle of Bob Dylan's songs and her own cries against what she called the establishment. She asked Bafemi to join in the call for love and muffle the guns of the establishment. Then she sent a large photograph of herself in a pose of pseudo-meditation. On the back of the photograph she inscribed 'I love you!' and drew the trendy sign of 'peace'. So much was Bafemi assailed by her correspondence that he could not help sending her a post-card, on which he wrote: 'We made lust, not love.' After that, she did not write.

Now on the train, Bafemi remembered Althea, Woli and Bayo. Woli represented the progression towards virtue. It was he who taught him many things early in life, and because of Woli's lessons, he could not agree with Althea's ideals. Bayo stood for the progression towards the physical perfection called beauty. Bayo taught him that the creation of beauty could only come when the artist reacted to the divine creative impulse. Pure creative expression, he said, came only when the artist had experienced his own phoenix rite in the crucible. This Bafemi had never understood. Bayo told him that its understanding would come with the normal cycles of life. Yet, that night in the Jordan was not anywhere near beauty.

Soon, it was time for the evening meal, after which he was too excited to read or sleep. The train moved nearer to Jos.

On the platform Mary waited. She had arrived at the station an hour earlier. She walked up and down the platform, stopped and looked into the dark as if to conjure the appearance of the train. She expected her son to be a big boy, then, handsome in his father's image.

'It's so cold,' a Hausa woman commented and added 'I hope he will come with more kola this time.' She was expecting her husband.

'You trade in kola?' Mary asked.

'Yes. It's a petty trade. He goes to the south with the cattle and on his way back, he buys me kola. These days, thanks to the train, its quicker.'

'But it is late today.'

'Late? Not yet. You are expecting a relative?'

'My son.' Mary smiled inwardly.

'Good for you. It is the cold that bites my skin.'

'Yes, it is a bit chilly,' Mary said, and walked down the platform.

Then she heard the train's approach. The other people on the platform, either dozing or standing were now on the alert. As the train crawled into the station, the people surged forward. The silence broke into a din. Desperately Mary began to search with her eyes among the arrivals.

On the platform, suitcase in hand, Bafemi waited patiently.

'You have not seen her?' the station master asked.

'Not yet,' Bafemi answered.

'When the platform clears up, you'll locate her ... Is she the lady in the raincoat?'

'No.' Bafemi was gripped by sudden anxiety. He sincerely wished that his mother would be there to welcome him.

Mary reached the other end of the platform, still searching anxiously with her eyes. Her heart beat faster. She wondered if she had misread his father's telegram. She walked down the platform again. It still teemed with people.

'You have not seen her yet?' the station master asked Bafemi who was then very anxious.

Mary heard the question and looked over the shoulder of a passer-by. She saw Bafemi.

'Bafemi!' She grabbed him and hugged him. The station master disappeared into the other side of the big station. She embraced him again. There were effusions of several sentiments. Mother and son went home in a taxi.

'Did you eat well in the train?'

'Yes. I was in the first class. His woman paid.'

'His mistress, Sulola?'

'You know her?'

'I am well informed, my dear. I also heard that he is redeveloping her village. I have people who give me the news. Don't let's talk about it now. After you have settled down, tomorrow or the day after we shall talk. Satisfied, darling?'

Everyone indulged and fondled him. The homely atmosphere at his grandparents' was a sharp contrast to his father's house in the south. Mary insisted that Bafemi should sleep on the bed, while she and Ayodele slept on a large mat on the floor. They all felt the flame of joy dance in their hearts, for the first time in years.

Ayodele spent the next two days constantly in her brother's company. She asked several questions about their father and expressed her desire to go back to the south with Bafemi. Her mother promised her a trip in the near future. On the third day the mother called her son to the long-awaited talk.

'Sit down, Bafemi. You are no longer a child. You are old enough now to understand things. And it seems your priest teacher has made an adult of you. That is your advantage in the present circumstances . . .'

The boy put in, 'I know, Mami. That's what everybody says. Woli does his duty, why do you refuse to do yours?'

'Don't you understand, darling? All right, I know that you want me to go back to your father now that his little wife Mope has left. I would like to go back too. So would your sister Ayodele. But, Bafemi, does your father want me to come back? Does he? I have suffered enough because of my love for a home. Your father does not care, Bafemi. It is to him you should talk.'

'Will you marry again? I asked you that the last time you came to Ibadan.'

It was then she told him about Seyidi. Up till then, none of them had mentioned Seyidi, neither had the Doctor himself paid a visit.

'So Uncle Seyidi is not my uncle? He is not one of your distant relatives?'

'We referred to him as Uncle Seyidi in the letters as a mere polite expression.'

'Mami, you mean you will marry him?'

'I have not given my answer, Bafemi. I agreed to a waiting period of a year. My answer is due in three months' time.'

'No! No, Mami, not you too!'

'Be reasonable, Bafemi. Look at me. Have I not suffered enough? Even then, anything may still happen between now and three months. I will grant all your father's demands in the divorce. If he really wants me back, he will show it. But I doubt it, Bafemi. Let us face reality! I have no other choice than my line of action.'

'What do you mean, you have no choice?' he yelled.

'Bafemi, don't shout at me,' she said gently. 'try to understand.'

'I am sure it is Uncle Seyidi prompting your present action.'

'Bafemi!'

'And all the while I thought you were better than Father. You are both the same. Selfish! You are not ready to consider us, the children.'

'Won't you forgive me and give me the freedom to make my own choice?'

'There is nothing to forgive, nothing to release into freedom. What about us, the children? For us there is no home, no proper home! Father has had a second failure. Perhaps he will have another trial. And you, you will build yours with *Uncle* Seyidi. Good for you and father. The trouble is that children never do have any choice. Anyway I am out of your family, you hear me? Out!'

Bafemi was resolved. Not once after that night did he look with a forgiving eye at his mother. She searched in vain for a loving look but all she got back, each time, was an acid gaze.

By coincidence Seyidi was busy at the hospital and Bafemi never saw him. He cut his stay short, very drastically. His grandparents could not persuade him to stay longer. He told Ayodele that he would come again. He knew in his heart that sooner or later his sister would understand that no proper home existed for them.

Mary saw her son move away from her. A gulf now existed between them. She prayed that he would forgive her. When the south-bound train was ready to move,

Bafemi embraced his sister warmly and gave his mother a hug. He got into the train. It gathered speed and quickly separated the boy from his sister and mother.

Emancipation was the word that formed the key to Bafemi's new approach to life. He looked back on his life and saw himself bound in chains. The home, the family, in this mental conception was that prison, from which his self asked for a total, uncompromising emancipation. There would be no tears, no remorse, no soft emotions. Life was now to be conquered.

He waited for the elevator on the top floor of Omolere Departmental Stores. Under his right arm was a large polythene bag, filled with what he considered the best of his paintings. His first move was to sell his paintings. All the paintings he had done recently, and the ones he had earlier marked fo the coming Arts festival, were to be sold. He evacuated the first batch from his small studio at home and came to discuss terms with the Sales Manager of Omolere Stores. He took this move two days after his return from the north.

'Bafemi!' A female voice was calling him. It was Althea. She ran to him.

'Hi, Althea.'

'Hi. I got your postcard and I have been thinking since then, you know. I think you are right. I have stopped going to Jordan, I'm going straight now. Ever heard of *The Path of the Grace*?'

His face lit up. She showed him a book she had just bought.

'It is the new literature I am reading. You know, getting there without drugs. It's all right. It's good literature, that.'

Bafemi became more fascinated by her.

'It's this author's second book and it's okay, you know. Where are you going?'

'Oh, er, I am selling my paintings.'

'Why?'

'I need cash and I want to leave home, that's why. I reject parental oppression, mental or otherwise.'

She looked at him for some time.

'I knew about parental oppression long before you. I am simply pissed off with my parents. That was how I went down the road, up to Jordan, and now I'm easing out of the scene. It all began with your post-card.'

Bafemi thought of the Grace and wondered if she understood what it meant. Althea's dress was more sober and it was remarkably clean. The Grace was the presence of the Divine, according to Woli's lessons. Yet somehow, Bafemi was increasingly finding it difficult to reconcile the beauty of the Grace with the negative phase he had been going through.

'I know a learned healer who once taught me for many years, what the Lord's Prayer was about and it gave me an insight into the Grace.'

'My friends think I am a crank, Bafemi. Maybe we should get together ... My intentions are pure, I promise.' She smiled. 'Come, let's go to my place.'

Bafemi had an appointment with the sales manager of Omolere Stores in two hours' time. He accepted Althea's invitation and they went to her place.

Althea, an only child was still rebelling against her mother, whom she referred to as one of the demagogues of the establishment. Her mother was a dental surgeon. Her father was a food expert in an international humanitarian organisation. He was always globe-trotting, negotiating for food for disaster-stricken areas of humanity. Althea regarded her father as an opportunist in the establishment, a pig in an *Animal Farm*. And Althea chose a part of the servant quarters for her little dwelling place, which she referred to in conversation as *The Shelter*.

On a wall of her small room, was an out-dated poster of *Free Angela Davis*. On another wall was one that demanded liberty for humanity in chains. That was a satirical poster. On a third wall was the bold graceful picture of Jesus Christ. The caption read; 'I love you, Jesus, you are the Superstar.'

The afternoon talk between Althea and Bafemi ranged between accusations against the pigs of the establishment and what she called the pure socialism of Jesus, the Christ.

'I will soon be off dope completely. It's a good thing I had not gone too far. When I leave school this year, I'll do some social work, help the poor and all that ... get away from here, live among the villagers and help them. And then I will study yoga, and read more of the Grace. What do you think, Bafemi?'

'I can't give you a perfect answer now. I have been out of discipline for a long time. If you want to meet Woli I can take you to him, and maybe the women can lead you into what you want. The Adept once told me that there is no end to the stewardship of the Grace ... But look, Althea, I have my new life to face.'

'It's part of it, isn't it?'

'I couldn't tell you. I suppose I still need the Grace as much as you.'

Althea fried *dodo* for him, as a lunch snack. She spoke endlessly against the puppets of the state and the pigs of the establishment. She said any nation that had no proper homes was damned. She said the establishment would die from the inside. She said she was 'pissed off' by the new craze for money and eventually she saw herself as a possible Joan of Arc, one day.

The truth was that Althea was seeking a permanent equilibrium. Like many of her age she was appalled by the extreme materialism of society, and she was instinctively reacting against the apathy of a decadent subculture. She reacted to the impulse of the age. It was an impulse of the spiritual. Many groups and sects were rising among the youth, crossing the barriers of many creeds of religion, and the only spectacular factor was their belief that their truth had never at one time existed upon the face of the earth. The danger for one like Althea was of swinging from her present extreme to the other one of the fanatic. Bafemi's past lessons from the Adept still proved their positive points. They no longer contained anything of the spectacular for the boy. They had become a part of the dual structure upon which, Woli said, the essence of man was created. This duality sprang from what he called *One* and in man it became *two*, the physical and its directing creative energy, which was infinite in character.

Bafemi was therefore surprised by Althea's zeal. He found her rebellion strangely irreconcilable with the profound peace of the girls working at the Adept's as the virgins of the Grace.

'Take me there, Bafemi. When will you have the time?' she asked.

'Not for the next few days.'

'Promise you'll call again.'

'I will. By the way, have you seen Deji lately?'

'No, not since I dropped out of the scene. I heard he will be having a party in a few days' time. His parents are going on a summer flight to the U.S. My own tyrants are also off to Britain in two days' time, for two months. Then I should be utterly alone . . . '

'I must go, Althea. I'll see you later.'

'Please do. And good luck with the paintings.' She gave the salute of peace. He responded in the same fashion, and left.

He was surprised that a post-card could change someone's way of life. He remembered the lone sentence of the post-card: 'We made lust, not love.'

It might have been part of a poster. He thought of the commercial viability of poster designing for publishing companies. He took a taxi back to Omolere Stores and saw the sales manager.

The manager did not accept the paintings because, according to him, he had exhausted the quarterly budgetary vote on such wares. The manager suggested Bayo Cole's popular gallery. Bafemi left and took another taxi to Bayo's studio. Bayo was away at work at the Ministry of Culture. Three hours passed before the artist came. His apprentice appealed for his help.

Bayo looked at each of the works critically.

'Bafemi, I'd prefer a super and solo exhibition for you in two years' time. You know that the kola-nut that is well hidden under the leaves ripens well. Two more years will reveal the genius in you. The gallery will launch you. Be more patient. We have to learn the virtue of patience in this vocation.'

'Why can't I have an exhibition now, Cousin Bayo?'

'It's not time yet, Bafemi. Win more trophies at the junior arts festival. Your success is assured beyond that. Be patient. What's the rush for anyway?'

'I need money.'

'You need money? Incredible. What's all Dr Sotomi's cash for? You amaze me.'

'If you won't take them, I'll hawk them.'

'That would spoil not only your reputation, but your family name.'

That got Bafemi and his ego suddenly rose to vain heights. He protested: 'I don't want any part of that rotten and piggish family! I hate it, do you hear? I hate it like shit! They are all pigs.'

'Bafemi!'

'Don't say anything. It's a rotten set up and I won't have anything to do with them.'

He took the polythene bag that contained the paintings and ran out. The artist was dumbfounded. He made to follow his apprentice, but stopped, hoping that the creative urge in the boy would be brought under control. As an afterthought he rang Dr Tunji Sotomi at home. They had a brief talk on Bafemi's new attitude.

Bafemi did not head for home. He took the Bodija residential areas as his first area of trial. There he went from door to door, hawking paintings. He was menaced by neurotic dogs, turned away by suspicious housewives and sneered at by others who told him to go and do an honest job. He sold nothing.

Since his return from the north, Bafemi became more reserved. He did not communicate with his father and completely disregarded Solula. Tunji quietly observed Bafemi and pretended not to know about his hawking exercises. He did not tell his son that Mary had finally sent the legal papers that would facilitate the divorce.

On the particular day that Tunji hoped to speak to his son, Sulola was summoned to Odo-Ode for a meeting with the village patriarchs. She drove down when the sun was on the decline, arrived at Odo-Ode in time for the meeting. She went into her uncle's Council Chamber where the patriarchs were seated, the elderly women at their feet. When Sulola had entered and sat down on a mat on the floor, the meeting began. It was a crucial patriarchal consultation on the authority of the new community whose genesis was to be declared in the next full moon.

The debate, in the meeting of the patriarchs and the mothers, was on the question of the new authority of the forthcoming Odo-Ode commune. They had received governmental support, and all that was required of them was the collective payment of tax. Yet, the people felt an urgent need for a definitive nucleus of authority. Authority, they argued should not be made up of only an economic unit, neither should it be policed in any way. In the days of old, what resembled the kind of authority they now required was the authority of the priest-king.

In the present, there was an urgent need for the age-old economic policy that could only be explained by the axiom: 'The soil yields to him who tills it. The earth appreciates the gifts of heaven in harvests.' The argument in the meeting was centred on how to ensure a complete departure from the old council power structure which represented the city in the village. Would the family with the large plot of land now lord it over the less fortunate? If so, what was the basis of communal equality?

'Obatala', the elder patriarch said, 'took the word from Olodumare and created the humans of the world. His creation came in many kinds and moods. Rich, poor, weak and strong, short and tall, large and narrow. But Adimula told us when his work was done, that all beings were equal. Our fathers did that before Ogun led them to the first wars and land became the privileged property of conquerors. Conquests have never given us the equality that Obatala asks of us.'

The other grey heads nodded, their mouths and

beards moving imperceptibly.

'We believe that those who have known the core of the earth should hold the power and distribute the wealth,' a lean elder said. 'With of course the advice of our mothers.'

'I give my respects to my fathers, my mothers, the ancestors and may the ripe spirits of the unborn guide my tongue.' Sulola knelt in the middle of the patriarchal circle. 'Of the rites of the core of the earth I know nothing. However I know that my blood has fed the earth before I became a woman. I feel like the earth. I know of fertile periods and the phases of drought, but I bear it like our mothers have taught me. I am a woman like the earth. I am yet to know of fruitful harvests.'

Her argument was that authority did not need to be in the hands of an exclusive few. It was felt that a grand council of family heads be chosen, or the oracle be consulted for the choice of the earth and the heavens, so that the commune would have the grace of the gods and live in eternal cycles.

Ogbo Imule, the head of those who 'knew' the secrets of the earth, stood up and spoke:

'We are the fathers of the tribe. The Oracle made us Ogbo Imule. Ogbo, if you do not understand what it means, is that cosmic age which is ripe enough to rule. It has nothing to do with only the earthly old. Look among us. Those who the oracle chose to be Ogbo Imule are both old and young. When we rule, the old and young rule, the oracle rules too.'

The others nodded and acquiesced speechlessly. Sulola greeted the elders again and pleaded:

'Let us consult the oracles for the new Odo-Ode. When the new moon appears, it is a new cycle. My fathers it is also a new beginning, a fresh beginning and we need a fresh consultation like one does for the initiation of the new women. The earth is a woman. The heaven is a man. The two create together. This is how you teach us. Let us perform the rites for the new Odo-Ode, the new woman.'

The council nodded again, agreeing with her. Ogbo

Imule got to his feet.

'It is true you helped us bring this new project. You rescued the farms. We live again. My daughter, you should not tell us what to do when it comes to ruling. The eyes of Ogbo see more than the eyes of Ogberi. We know what we are talking about.'

Sulola was reminded that she was in fact not a major initiate of any sort. The rites she knew were the ordinary female rites of circumcision and the minor initiation into womanhood. She gave Ogbo Imule an acid gaze and held it for long, unflinching.

The cultist head spat bitterly and said: 'The earth is a respectable woman. Do you think you are her respectable daughter? Go and wash before you come back to address us.'

Sulola rose to her feet, a taboo in the pressence of the elders. The women rebuked her with their strong eyes. She defied them. She eased up her tension slowly, already mentally reciting her minor initiation incantation, throwing every word with force. It gave her the strength she needed.

She turned to her uncle, the village head, and said: 'I regret that I will not be part of a commune ruled by any closed cult. I give you my respects, my mothers.' She curtsied.

'Which wind do you think will bear you home, child?' Ogbo Imule asked. 'Do you think the wind of the evening will bear you home when you disrespect your very source?'

Sulola faced Ogbo Imule squarely, taking his visual focus in hers, boldly. She recited the incantation mentally, with fervour.

'Even in any storm of disaster, Ofe will bear me home. *Ma dele dandan.*' She retorted that her boat would definitely put to shore.

Ogbo Imule spat. Sulola spat and left the meeting. The desecration was total. The women muttered: '*Asasi!*' Baba pleaded for calm. In the ensuing confusion Ogbo Imule took his metal sceptre of office and cursed, pronouncing the verb, whose essence was' the most destructive element of *asasi*.

Sulola headed for Ibadan, her foot flat on the accelerator of the Mercedes Benz.

> I turn with the month, I turn with the
> moon
> When I am half like the moon, the
> earth fills me,
> I empty myself with the moon in the
> fields after harvest.
> Protect me wholly, hide me fully, me,
> A seed of the earth, to give the fruits
> of tomorrow.
> I am a woman like you ... '

Again and again she went through the verse as she was taught so many years ago. It was, she was told like the other girls, a powerful protective incantation.

The night grew dark. The headlamps of the Mercedes parted the darkness keenly. She negotiated the bends with calm and took the straights with boldness. The heavy car sped through the night. Sulola felt her loneliness. Her heart longed for a reassuring companion. Repeatedly she recited the incantation.

> A seed of the earth, fed in darkness,
> Opening with pain, in the bud of
> future fruits.
> *Ma dele dandan*!

The car took the narrow bridges with complete risks, ran over the bumps without care. The woman behind the wheel fled, as if from a most potent evil. The night loomed still, ahead with its dark. The trees stood on the roadsides pronouncing the largeness and hugeness of night. Night birds hit the car and dropped dead or dizzy.

The distance grew less and diminished further until the lights of Ibadan appeared. The car began a descent down the road.

> *Ma dele dandan*!

When it happened, Sulola did not know. In a flash she hit the ditch and the car tumbled over. The door flew open with a force that flung her a few feet away. She landed on soft shrubbery, coldly unconscious.

No one saw the accident, because there was no one on the road then.

Sulola's subconscious brought forth her dead sons, tugging at her wrap, as in her poor former days, asking her for food. They tugged and tugged. She asked them to let her be and she regained consciousness. The dew was wet on her skin. A few leaves hung over her face. Like an automaton, she rose and looked towards the road. She clambered back on the road. Slowly she realised what had happened. She had had an accident. Curiously no bone was broken, but her leg was bleeding from a cut. She looked at her watch. It said eight. It was very dark. She began the long trek back to town. A cargo truck came along and she hitched a ride, saying nothing to the driver and his mate. She only thanked God and them. In these parts people knew what this type of experience meant.

'Abi you want to go hospital, madam?'

'No, I am going home first . . . ' She groaned.

'Pele, you alone, madam?'

'Yes. Luckily yes.'

'Na God save you. Make you Saraa to God.'

They dropped her in front of Tunji's house. She thanked them and rang the bell. Tunji opened it.

'Sulola! . . . What happened?'

'Oh I'm glad to be back. It's those fools at the village . . . I had an accident.'

'You look terrible!'

Sulola stretched herself on the divan. The doctor was called. She was treated for shock. Her wound was dressed. She was told to have a long rest. She cleaned herself up and sent Tunji's houseboy for a change of clothes from her house.

'Stay here tonight, Sulola.'

'You bet I will.'

Towards eleven, she had regained her calm and had a

soft drink. Tunji had also heard the whole story. He named the day a day in which many things happened. Towards midnight he went to Bafemi's small studio. The boy was painting there. Tunji called him, thinking it was also time to advise his son. Sulola was relaxed, from the effects of tranquillisers. She lay on the divan half-asleep. It started to rain outside.

'Bafemi, have a soft drink and then go to bed. It's late enough. Continue your painting tomorrow since you are on holiday.'

Tunji gave his son a glass of orange drink. Without knowing why Sulola was in the house, Bafemi hated her on sight.

'Bafemi, how true is it that you are now hawking paintings?' Tunji saw the defiant glare on his son's face and because of Sulola, the father toned down his voice. 'Is it true, Bafemi? You should not tramp the town like a hungry vagabond.'

'I am not a vagabond, much less a hungry one.'

'I asked you a simple question. Did you hawk paintings?'

'Yes.'

'You should not do that, you know. You have all you want. A small studio, lots of artist's equipment, and every other thing. Besides, it will be a stain on the family name if you hawk paintings. Have you ever heard a Sotomi do that sort of thing . . . Please, Bafemi.'

Bafemi raised the half-full glass of orange in the air and smashed it against the wall:

'Don't talk to me about any family! I am sick and tired of so much talk of a family that does not exist.'

Sulola stared in amazement. Tunji was horrified.

'Bafemi, will you control yourself.'

'There is nothing to control. I will do what I like, hawk paintings and anything else.'

Sulola intervened in a weak voice: 'Tunji, keep this till tomorrow. Let him go to bed.'

'Stay out of this, you shameless whore!' Bafemi yelled. His father rushed at him and knocked him down with a vicious slap across the face.

'She loves you, don't you know, you senseless child!'

Bafemi scrambled up and sneered: 'Pigs.' In three bounds the boy opened the door and went into the rain outside. The boy tucked his hands in his pockets and went through the rain. A thunderclap resounded in the sky. The boy did not show any concern for the rain. For all he cared, buckets of rain could fall from the sky and flood the earth. He desired a total unleash of the bolts of the clouds and wished for multiple self-beating mortars of thunder. He was not bothered if the sheets of rain beat through his clothes and hit into his bones.

What mattered then was his feeling of emancipation.

Soon, he realised that he was walking to Deji's. As he approached the house of Deji's parents, red lights glowed unmistakably from afar. The apprentice then remembered that Althea had mentioned Deji's proposed party. Bafemi wanted to turn back but he felt an immediate need for shelter. He walked slowly towards the house.

Deji exclaimed when he saw him: 'Couldn't you ring that you were coming to the party? The old man's car is at my disposal now. You should not have got so wet.'

Bafemi said nothing. Deji propelled him to a room, threw fresh clothes at him. 'Get dressed and join the party.' Bafemi changed slowly, feeling cautious, without knowing why. It was a disturbing premonition that he felt. So he sat on a chair, after getting dressed. The wild music of the party reached him.

Ten

Deji breezed into the room: 'Hey man, what's wrong with you? This is a party and we are all together. My ma and pa are away on holiday. Come on, man, it's all together ... Togetherness, man! Togetherness!'

Deji gave Bafemi a cool glass of soft drink and dragged him out of the room. Bafemi drank down the whole glass, without knowing that the drink had been mixed with dope. The large room of the party had no furniture, except for the stereo-set booming from a corner. The young people, the same old regulars of Jordan, either stood or sat on the floor, in lotus style, swaying to the music. Bafemi sat, determined not to be a party to any of their usual orgy. He looked round the room and felt glad that Althea was not there.

One of the lights was put out. A new disc was put on the set and was greeted by cat-calls. As the crooning voice of the vocalist came up, amidst twangs of guitar and bang-bang-bang of drums, the boys and girls chorused with a single heavy word:

'Togetherness!'

Three girls went on the floor, dancing, arms flailing, their forms gyrating, their backsides purposely jigging.

'Togetherness!'

Three boys joined the other trio and they became three couples, tightly merged together. Bafemi felt some hollowness in his stomach. His head felt light. Another bulb of light went out. The room became darker.

'Togetherness!'

Deji took a girl to the floor. The dancing forms increased. Soon it became obvious what the long play disc was about. Its song, percussions and melodies led only to the erotic sensations. As it began its climax with all kinds of suggestive rhythms, which left little to one's imagination, the young people began to strip, slowly.

The disc dictated the pace.

'Togetherness!'

Bafemi felt his head floating away from his body as the initial effects of L.S.D. made themselves felt. Everything was changing its form in perpetual motion. On the floor, to his vision, it was Sodom incarnate that he beheld.

'To – ge – therness!'

Three girls were completely naked, running around the room, doing hide and seek among other human forms, giggling and laughing. Bafemi cocked his head to one side and thought he saw dogs chasing each other. The dogs changed their forms to humans as they wished. He shook his head weakly.

'To – getherness!'

Then the girls made for Bafemi, giggling. They began to paw him, kiss him. He thought he was being licked by some female dogs, reacting to heat. He fought back. An ensemble of daemonic laughter rang in his head. He could not see that it was Deji giving the girls a helping hand, stripping him. Bafemi was now completely in the void between reality and illusion, the medium of transition that the youthful subculture termed a 'trip'. In the realm of illusion, a 'good trip' was heaven to this decadent youth, while a 'bad trip' was hell. Bafemi was having a bad trip.

'Together – ness!'

Bafemi kicked violently, shouting 'Dogs! Pigs! Lay off me! Pigs!' He knocked the girls over. They continued to giggle.

'Shake it off, man. Cool it, man. Cool it!' Deji was shaking Bafemi by the shoulders. Bafemi hit wildly at Deji. He missed, sprawled on his face. His hand touched a bottle. Bafemi grabbed the empty bottle, struggling to his feet. He swayed and hit the bottle against the wall. In his present realm of illusion, what he saw assailing him were laughing dogs of hell.

'I'll kill you dogs! I'll kill you!'

Deji was shouting: 'Cool it, man. Cool it, baby. Cool it!' The girls began to scream. The music stopped. In his dilated vision, Bafemi saw the horde of dogs zoom towards him. He swung the broken bottle round, yelling: 'I'll kill you, before you get me, dogs!'

Deji got another idea. He took two bottles of iced water from the fridge and splashed it on Bafemi's face. While the boy was stunned, they rushed and disarmed him. Deji began to slap Bafemi on the face, until the tripping boy became submissive. Deji propelled him downstairs, helped by two friends. They quickly put on some clothes, and pushed Bafemi into the car belonging to Deji's parents.

Upstairs the party resumed. The rites of orgy were reset.

Deji started the car nervously. One of the boys asked him:

'Are you okay, Deji?'

'Yeah, I'm cool, man. Real cool.' He swung the car on the road.

'Where do we take him?' the boy asked Deji.

'Not to his old man anyhow. I know a chick who might put him up. Althea her name is. She digs him, digs him fine. She's a cool chick. So he'll be all right.'

'It's a bad trip.'

'Yeah, I know,' Deji said. 'Hell, it's probably his first. I thought Althea must have taught him how. Wasn't my fault. Was it? Hell, man. I'm cool, man.'

'It's okay, man,' the other boy reassured Deji. They laughed nervously.

They reached Althea's. Deji knocked on Althea's shelter.

'Who is it?'

'It's Deji. It's me, Althea. Open! It's urgent. Althea!'

'Go away.'

'Althea, I've got Bafemi with me and he's really sick. Baby, Althea, open up.'

'Oh, shut up!' She opened the door. Deji and the two boys carried Bafemi in. Deji gave a nervous and incomprehensible account of what had happened.

'Please keep him, Althea. He will recover soon.' Deji escaped into the night with his accomplices. Althea took another look at Bafemi and pitied him. The boy was delirious and shivering. She laid him on the bed and stripped him, then slipped on him a pair of her own pyjamas. She made some hot water and diluted it. She set to bathe his feet with a warm wet towel. Gently, she did it until she was satisfied that he was better. She then massaged his feet with a balm and put a coverlet over him.

Bafemi's stomach heaved in his present placid state. He jerked up, bent over and gushed forth a pool of vomit.

'What have they done to you? Oh, what have they done to you?' Althea started to clean up the mess patiently. She removed the messy coverlet and covered him with another cloth. She rubbed a balm on his forehead. Later she made him a mixture of warm water and lime and gave it him to drink. He drank it, all in a dreamy state. Morning was breaking when he became silent and slept. She slept on the chair.

In the morning she cleaned the room while he still slept. Towards dusk he woke up. She sat beside the bed, dutifully.

'Althea?' he said weakly. 'Althea?'

'Yes, Bafemi, it's me. You have been very ill.'

He looked round and demanded what he was doing in her room. Althea told him to rest, since they could discuss it later. He closed his eyes and felt a bottomless pit of hunger in his stomach.

'Althea?'

'Yes, Bafemi.'

'I feel so weak and hungry. Famished.'

She laughed and disappeared into the kitchen of her shelter. She put on some rice on the gas fire. She prepared some pepper soup. Soon Bafemi was eating a refreshing meal. Then Althea told him how he was brought to her in the middle of the night. She told him that Deji had left for Lagos. He telephoned in the afternoon. Bafemi stood up and took some firm steps round the room. He looked out, through the window. Slowly he pieced the events of the previous day together, up till when he took what he referred to as the cup of poison. He sighed.

'You need more rest, Bafemi.'

'I know. It seems so difficult now that I have my own affairs in my own hands. And only God can save Deji when next I see him ... ' He groaned. 'I need help, Althea. I need help. I feel so tired and helpless.'

He told her that he had left home finally. His hope was on the sales of his paintings.

'Will you help me, Althea? I have nowhere to stay.'

'You can stay here. My own tyrants are away on holiday for the next six weeks.'

'Good. I only need time to sell enough paintings and earn money for my school fees before we resume in three weeks' time.'

She promised to help. He went back to bed. She waited on him, reading her copy of *The Path of the Grace*.

Tunji stood looking at the door through which Bafemi had gone into the rainy night. Sulola sighed and closed her eyes. It was no use going after him in the storm. Tunji guessed that his son might have gone to Woli's or Bayo Cole's studio or even to Mama. He asked Sulola to go to bed and assured her that the situation was not out of hand.

Sulola went to sleep in the guest room. On her mind was the argument with the elders of Odo-Ode. The launching of the commune was now in the balance. Regarding Bafemi's revolt, she had some sympathy for the boy and wished to get out of Tunji's life completely before she became too embroiled in his problems.

In the office Tunji rang Bayo. Bafemi was not there. Further enquiries were made during the ensuing hours. Bafemi was not at Mama's nor at Woli's. Tunji's concern and worries increased.

Before he left the office, a message came from Odo-Ode that work had ground to a halt, following a decision made by the village elders.

The new commune of Odo-Ode was not going to be launched. In one whole view, Tunji saw the dream of his grand ambition crash. The only remaining hope was to persuade the elders to launch their commune on the basis of an economic nucleus. The possibility of the elders accepting that suggestion was remote. It was the collective view of the Odo-Ode that the only basis for oneness should be spiritual, which mattered more than the material.

On the question of authority, the exoteric group of Ogbo Imule insisted on an absolute monopoly. Indeed, from the time of their genesis, authority, as handed down from the fountain-head of the tribe, was dual in Odo-Ode. Authority was exoteric and esoteric. One was a reflection of the other. Centuries of corruption and warfare turned the esoteric into a terror gang, while the exoteric was replaced by the modern forms of administration. It would be an enormous task to destroy such a cult as Ogbo Imule, if Odo-Ode was to have a fresh genesis. Old Baba, the Bale, told the people to go back to their old ways of farming while the question of authority was endlessly being debated.

The possible collapse of Tunji's pet dream added to his anxiety. He did not see Sulola who was having a rest cure. By evening it was apparent that Bafemi was missing. Tunji had a sleepless night, alone with the houseboy in the house. Vaguely he felt the absence of life in his wonder-house. In the morning, Mope entered with her son, as defiantly as ever.

She had brought her son to stay in Tunji's house. The child was, she argued, old enough to live with him. In reality, as the child grew older he became more of a hindrance to Mope in her pursuit of illicit commerce with men. The reputation of her generosity grew and attracted a boom which made her decide to bring along her son and leave him with Tunji, irrespective of the consequences.

'But I have been paying to the Welfare regularly,' Tunji argued.

'Will money give him the paternal care he needs? He will stay with you, no matter what you say or do.'

'I have no housemaid to take care of him.'

'That is your headache. Not mine. The son is ours. Do

you think that a child belongs only to the mother? It is our shared responsibility, sir.'

'Mope, be reasonable. You cannot just drop him on me without warning. I am a very busy man.'

She hissed and said: 'Once you said I had no claim to you, except the child. So here is the child, your only claim. Take him!' She went out of the house, back to her trade of lascivious pleasures.

Tensions grew in Dr Tunji Sotomi. He rang up Sulola and asked how she was. He told her of Bafemi's flight into an unknown hideout. He related the new development to her. Sulola promised to help, and arrived a few hours later, looking lean from fatigue. Again she reminded him of his duties to the home. It was the home that mattered before any other thing. She repeated her wish for a complete departure from his life in the immediate future.

'Sulola, you must stay with me. I need your help more than ever.'

'I am not a woman to be owned by any man. You demand too much from me, Tunji. I cannot stay any longer when your son returns. I have known more love since I met you, and I have also known more tensions. Sadly enough, Odo-Ode is becoming an abortive venture. Tunji, I am becoming wearied.'

'You can take a holiday after Bafemi is found. But you will come back to me.'

'No, Tunji, I need more than a holiday. I need complete repose. The failure of Odo-Ode and the events of the recent past demand a complete seclusion.'

'Sulola . . .'

'Enough, Tunji, I am simply weary.'

She began to play with Mope's son. Tunji rang the office to say he would arrive late. He sat down to consider the several ways through which he could find Bafemi and call him home. The police, he felt, should not be told in order to prevent any publicity that might scandalise his name. The police would only be called in if all other ways proved impossible. On the evening of that day, he decided to employ the services of the taxi-driver's union. Bafemi's passport photograph would be printed and distributed as the first step of Tunji's private detection. This he hoped would determine if the boy was still in Ibadan.

Bafemi was better physically on the third day. He informed Althea of his plan to steal into his father's house and remove his paintings, as well as some of his immediate requirements.

'It's risky, Bafemi. I don't want them to catch you. We must not let the establishment get us. You know that they must suffer more. Don't go yet. Your father may have told the police – the pigs.'

'I don't think he has. It would have been put in the newspapers as a public announcement. My father is too proud of his family name to do that now. Later, yes, but not now. I'll go, Althea.'

In the mid-morning Bafemi took a taxi which dropped him a short distance from his father's house. The taxi-driver looked at the printed photograph in the handbill he had received earlier from his union. He noticed the resemblance and turned his taxi immediately in the direction of his union headquarters.

Bafemi stood in front of the back door of the house and brought out his own key. He paused with doubt. Then he turned the key in the lock with a burglar's stealth. He strained his ears for the slightest sound. He went in and shut the door firmly, but quickly. The thick carpeting of the house made it easy for him to walk without any noisy footsteps. He went into his studio. The polythene bag was there, untouched and unransacked. The boy managed to put two other paintings into the bag. He took as many paint brushes as he could. He could not take any money from his room, since his father kept his post-office savings book. He left the studio, and went back the way he came.

At the exit, he heard Sulola's voice and turned round.

'Have you forgotten the burglar alarm system of your own father's house?' she asked.

He remembered and noticed that the house music was off. In its place was high sonic buzz, equally musical, but with an intermittent long alarming whine. Bafemi was a few feet from the exit. Sulola was many feet away. He bolted for the door, ran out, slamming it behind him. His movement was hampered. He chose a hedge of flowers, disappearing behind it and made for the adjacent street. He kept on walking fast. He looked behind him. There was no one chasing him. Too scared of being chased by Sulola in the car, he walked back to Althea, covering a distance of more than five miles. In the city it was easy to keep off the main road, following the labyrinths of ancient alleyways.

'But how did you let him get away?'

'He was near the door, Tunji, and did you expect me to go after him with Mope's son to look after?' Sulola said and added, 'Anyway, I have made arrangements for a housemaid. And, Tunji, I did not intend to force him to stay.'

'What?'

'Talk him home. That's all you can do if you don't want to apply police force which will only worsen matters. Thank goodness he is still in Ibadan anyway.'

'The taxi-drivers' union have traced him to this house. It is all tied up, Sulola. He still intends to hawk his paintings for a living. I will send for his mother. She has to know about this.'

During the next few days, Bafemi dropped completely out of sight, because he was painting. No report came in from the taxi-drivers. Distress took a complete hold on Tunji. Mary arrived the next week-end. Tunji and Bayo awaited her arrival at Mama's. It was a significant meeting between the separated husband and wife in view of the coming dissolution of their marriage.

Mary, whose anxiety had grown to a climax since she left Jos, could almost run into the house and ask what the reason for the urgent call was. The telegram simply asked her to come. She was not told that Bafemi had run away from home. Her mind examined all the possibilities of any relevant reason, but she vaguely felt that it had to do with Bafemi. She fearfully considered the possibility of death.

She tore into the sitting-room, where Mama, Bayo and Tunji waited. She went on her knees, as the traditional respect for Mama. Tearfully she asked, 'Is it my son? Is it Bafemi? What happened to him?'

Tunji was deeply embarrassed when his sister, Mama, looked at him, as if saying, 'There lies your responsibility.'

'It's Bafemi,' Tunji said.

Mary saw Tunji for the first time. It was their first meeting since he went to England, many years before.

'Tunji!' His voice remained the same to her ears. Her look was accusing, utterly unforgiving. 'Tunji! Tunji, have you now built all the homes of the nation, and all the communes, that you neglect your own home?'

Her tone was aggressive but lacking the sharp edge of violence. She gave him a very long look.

'The newspapers said so much about you. The band leaders sang your praises. At one time, I began to think you were ten times your size. Now you have driven our son to disaster!' She turned to Mama. 'Tell me, ma, is my son dead? I will take it . . .'

She made strong efforts not to cry.

'Mary, Bafemi is not dead. He ran away from home. Why and how do not matter now. We want him back and we feel you should be told about it.'

The people believed traditionally that a dead child was better than a missing one. For them there was more tragedy in missing a child, than in the child's death, because death was regarded as a necessary transition.

Mary was deeply distressed and she made Tunji see it in her very cold stare. Tunji spoke for the second time, explaining the stages of the investigations. It relieved Mary to learn that Bafemi was still alive in Ibadan. Mama comforted her and asked her to stay with her, hoping that Bafemi would soon be traced. Matters progressed that evening until Mama ensured a private meeting between the long separated husband and wife.

'How are your parents?' Tunji asked.

Mary said: 'They are well. They took care of me

when you drove me mad. Tunji, you are not a god, are you?'

'Don't talk like that.'

'How else can I talk? Bafemi simply will not adapt to your own style of life. He cannot see any cause for it.'

'You are marrying again, are you not? You have also sent me the papers for our divorce.'

'And you?'

'Me . . . Yes, I may marry again.'

Mary softened and regarded Tunji with plain eyes. She accused him. 'You have no reason for our separation and divorce, Tunji. Yet I have promised the man in my life an answer within the next two months. I do not know what answer to give. Not yet, I keep my mind open. It is a very long time, Tunji, but I believe that we could have built a home together . . . and perhaps, we still can . . .'

Tunji shifted in his seat. He had so much banked on Sulola's eventual consent that he felt it would be conflicting to answer Mary. To him, Mary's simplicity was no match for Sulola's sophistication, neither could Mary's quiet stand up against Sulola's sociability. It was all there in his subconscious. He did not add to what Mary said, and she took it for a negative answer. Later she said: 'We'll have to find Bafemi first and appeal to him to adjust . . .'

The long-separated husband and wife ended their conversation. Tunji went home, with Mary on his mind. The touching simplicity was still in her, that same simplicity which had attracted him at the very beginning during their courtship. It was curiously strange that is was the same quiet and simplicity he now refused to accept. He thought of the possibility of strong persuasion on Sulola. That night his sleep was interrupted by anxiety and doubts about his insistence on having a life of fun and fame, irrespective of the need for a home. Simply, society frowned on such men as he, for celibacy of any kind was regarded as the exclusive phase for young men up to the age of early twenties. Tradition demanded a respectable marriage from a man of his age. His thoughts went from Sulola to Mary. Once he flinched at the notion of the collapse of the Odo-Ode project. The E.C.E. was prosperous enough on common projects, but Odo-Ode would have been a national breakthrough.

One morning, during the days of anxious wait for Bafemi's return, two taxi-drivers brought the same message to Tunji's house. Bafemi had been dropped by the taxi-drivers in the premises of Omolere Stores. Sulola, now fully recovered from the shock of her motor accident, left Mope's son in the charge of the housemaid and followed Bafemi's trail. Meanwhile Tunji was having an uneasy board meeting at the office, concerning his official angle of the Odo-Ode project.

Sulola drove her second car, a Peugeot 505, to Omolere Stores, and parked at a strategic point at the car-park. She came out, wandered into the big super-market, came out later, wondering why on earth she was part of the Sotomi drama. Yet she persisted. She sat in the car. From there, she looked for the missing boy among the hawkers, now rushing at the departing customers of Omolere Stores.

Bafemi was nowhere to be found. However, Sulola noticed a slim girl in jeans, carrying a large polythene bag. She was obviously hawking paintings. Sulola observed Althea's movements and undying enthusiasm to sell the paintings. One or two expatriates appreciated two paintings, but no sale was made. Sulola got out of the car and approached Althea, carefully pretending she was not heading for her. Althea, who did not know Sulola, saw the woman and went to advertise her wares.

'Would you like to buy some nice African pictures, Madam?'

Sulola stopped and smiled. She examined two paintings.

'That one is called *Oya*, named after the goddess. And this one is *Ogunpa in Flood*.'

'Nice pictures. You painted them?'

'What ... er, no, as a matter of fact I am helping a brother. Don't you think they are really nice?'

'Yes, they are. How much do you sell each one for?'

'How many do you want?'

'Three or four.'

Althea chose four for Sulola.

'Altogether they are worth eighty ₦aira. You see, Madam, works like these cannot strictly be priced. Tomorrow when you come, they may be of higher value.'

Sulola got the four paintings from her.

Althea was excited and her elation could not be hidden.

'Tell me, perhaps your brother can do a painting of me. Where can I employ his services?' Sulola paid for the paintings.

'Really, madam?' Althea was mad with joy. 'In that case, I'll ask him. Can you let me know your address?'

'I am a business-woman, travelling through. I stay in a hotel, but I could meet him here tomorrow if you give me the time. Then I will book an appointment for my next trip to Ibadan.' Sulola smiled amiably.

'Fantastic. Really, Madam, our meeting is providential.'

'Indeed, my dear, indeed.'

'What's your name?'

'Althea ... Madam, meet us here tomorrow at eleven. Okay? Oh you're such a mother.'

'All right, Althea, tomorrow at eleven.'

Althea said goodbye and walked down the commercial street, her heart jumping with joy. Sulola smiled secretly to herself, went back to the car, drove home to her place. It was her decision to keep her discovery a secret, and reveal it later as a pleasant surprise. The following day she would ring Tunji at ten and ask him to come along. She believed that Althea was a certain lead to Bafemi.

That exceptional day brought an emotional relief for Bafemi. He questioned Althea more closely.

'Tell me, Althea, are you sure it was not a policewoman?'

'No!'

'It sounds so easy, that's all. Eighty Naira is a good start. But I don't think I will go. You should also stay away from that place for another week.'

'That leaves us a week before school resumes.'

'Yes. I need about thirty Naira more to pay for my fees and free myself from them completely.'

Althea's eyes were bright with triumph. She sat on the carpet, in the lotus position.

'We shall overcome, Bafemi.'

'But I am still afraid of what Father may do at school. They may throw me out of school and I don't want that. Why should I be forced to adapt to a situation that I hate? Why? I am not being obsessive, am I?'

'No. Thousands run away from home each year, getting away from their own tyrants. We shall overcome.'

Bafemi and Althea did not keep the appointment that Sulola went for. She felt thoroughly stupid. Tunji felt embarrassed and appreciated the fact that he had not brought Mary along to the car park, and that he did not have enough time to tell her. Sulola took it for her own failure.

'I was trying to help, Tunji. I was only trying to help. But clearly, it is time for me to make my exit from your life. Let our association now be strictly official in so far as the new Odo-Ode hangs on the balance. I love Bafemi dearly and he makes me regret my own childlessness.'

'Don't say that, Sulola.'

'It is a fact. I will help you with Mope's child, only if something urgent is needed. For the present, the housegirl will take care of him. Call back your wife, Tunji. I am a free woman . . . no pretence about it.'

'Mary is getting married again.'

'Pity. Anyway, I will take my exit. If and when Bafemi comes home, I shall make a final effort to give him my love. If he rejects it, it is my own lot.'

At that moment, Tunji felt lonely. Sulola entered her car and went back to her own business. Tunji got into his car, drove round the big city, feeling abandoned. His career, the fame he had built up was threatened by Odo-

Ode's indecision. His house, he realised, was not a home. Now he lacked, even the strength to throw himself back into the life of fancies that he had desired to have when he preferred to be a bachelor. He drove round the town, while many matters remained unattended to in the office. He remembered his thesis and its speculative ideals. The success of his thesis now seemed to be mere self-mockery because it was losing its past glory in the present Odo-Ode fiasco.

The days went by without any further reports of Bafemi's movements in Ibadan. Tunji made a last desperate decision. He went to the school principal of Bafemi and narrated the story of the flight from home. It was felt that Bafemi would still come to school, with his new sense of independence, and if he did, it was his parents' last hope of harmonising with him.

Althea withdrew all her savings from the post-office and gave it to Bafemi for the continuous struggle in the 'rebellion' against the tyrants of the home. In the brief interlude, Bafemi saw his own final hope of salvation in the annual scholarship competition. He decided to enter for it. For the last few days of his holidays he applied himself strictly to his studies, and refrained from going out.

Mary's hope, like Tunji's, was on the school opening day. Seyidi had a daily conversation with Mary on the telephone, boosting her morale.

The Adept, alone, was confident that the Grace would restore harmony. The artist, Bayo Cole, wondered endlessly if he was not to blame for refusing to exhibit the paintings of his apprentice.

Althea was a day student, while Bafemi had been a boarder. It was now his wish to become a day student, and find a private hostel to stay. The school reopened. Mary and Tunji went to the Government Academy to wait in the visitors' reception room of the school. Old Jones, the school principal, took charge of affairs on that opening morning.

Old Jones stood in front of his office watching the boys as they walked past and gave him a quick 'good morning'. The principal spotted Bafemi from a distance. Bafemi looked ahead, as if expecting nothing spectacular to happen. Old Jones did the same, putting on his usual air of the school administrator, concerned only with the school opening day. Bafemi came nearer. Old Jones responded mechanically to the greetings of his students. Bafemi reached the front of Jones's office.

'Bafemi Sotomi!'

The boy stopped and mumbled a quick 'good morning, sir'.

'Come in, my boy.' Jones said, turning to enter the office. Bafemi went after him with trepidation.

'Sit down,' Jones said. 'We are going to have some talk together. Because of that, the vice-principal will conduct the school assembly. First of all, why have you not reported back to the boarding house?'

'I am no longer a boarding student.'

'With whose permission?'

'I don't think I need permission to become a day student.'

'I see. With whose authorisation then?' the principal asked with his habitual patience. Bafemi gave no answer. Jones repeated the question.

'I did not know that it had to be authorised, sir,' Bafemi said.

'It has to be authorised by your father, boy. Officially you are still a boarding house student. You must go back home, get your things and come back into residence. If you want to be a day student, your father must make an application for that. This is a government school, a model for other schools. No behaviour of indiscipline will be tolerated, or you face suspension, or even expulsion.'

'I don't want to come back to the boarding house. I have no money for the fees.'

'Fees have nothing to do with you. That is your parents' concern.'

'I am now responsible for myself sir.'

Jones saw the determination on Bafemi's face. The school principal had been faced with cases of friction between parents and children several times and he had enough experience to mediate sensibly. Jones paced the length and breadth of the office.

'Why are you now responsible for yourself, my boy?'

Bafemi said nothing for a while, but having gained enough confidence from Jones's usual liberal attitude, he spoke again. 'There are many reasons, sir. I cannot explain them all.'

'However, perhaps you will explain them in the presence of your parents.' Jones called Dr and Mrs Sotomi into the office, from the adjoining reception room.

Relieved, Mary rushed at her son. Tunji thanked Jones, feeling a weight removed from his mind. Ironically it was the first time that Bafemi had ever seen his parents together. The sight of them together brought suggestions and the possibilities of a reconciliation to his mind. This melted the strand of revolt that he had previously been holding on to. He responded with warmth to them, assuming a total triumph over their own previous selfish decision.

It required only a few hours from the encounter, for Bafemi to realise that the couple had not come together. They came together only to search for him. After so many years of refusing to adapt himself to the separation of his parents, he decided to accept them as failures, but privately insisted on his own independence. Then he decided that it did not matter whether or not they re-married or remained separated; what concerned him was independence from their own state of failure. It only re-affirmed his earlier decision on his return from the north. He saw the next few years, before his higher school leaving certificate examinations, as the last phase of tolerance.

However, he hung on to the scholarship competition, which if he won, would make him sever his link completely with his parents, without qualms or regrets.

At this point, neither Bafemi nor anyone else realised that his obsession verged on a neurosis which began to rule and direct his passion for work and study.

Mary left for the north. Tunji resumed his ineffectual campaign for Odo-Ode. Sulola kept more to herself, suffering in the silent failure of Odo-Ode, expecting a delegation to recall her to a meeting of reconciliation with the elders. No delegation came. The constructions stood empty, without any life.

Althea shared Bafemi's dream with him and kept the earnings for the painting for him. Bafemi plunged into unceasing studies in preparation for the scholarship examination. A few days after being back in school, he withdrew to himself, and studied without a pause. Work became a schizophrenic therapy for him and he applied himself with frightening obsession. He ate less, mainly because he now lacked any appetite. The progress he made in his work did not slow him down.

Bafemi was suffering from obsession, which was indirectly an aggression channelled against his parents but which broke him down slowly. The boy was not aware of it. His mates took it for an act of determination to pass his scholarship exam.

The examination approached. As it came nearer, feverish application to work began to weaken the boy. Each day that passed gave him some triumph. He forgot to have his meals. He kept his sanitation to the minimum. The futile efforts to rebel during the past years all added up into one last heave which was tearing him up physically, as he psyched himself. No one noticed anything. It was not unusual for serious students to lose weight, neither was it unusual for them to hibernate.

The day before the examination Bafemi had the initial symptoms of fever. He ignored it. On the eve of the examination, he was too excited to sleep. He rose from the bed, with a zeal that contained a consuming and destructive fire. Bafemi without knowing it, kept that fire burning. He thought that he needed no meal, for his mouth felt sweet enough. He had only a glass of water. He went into the examination room.

His extreme eagerness for success, for victory over his parents, drove his sequences of thought and reason so that they gradually slipped away from the normal stream of logic. It was during the last paper that the sensation came to his head.

His head felt lighter, his vision sharper. When he started on his last paper, he had lost his sense of clarity. At the end he deluded himself and rejoiced in a victory which was not existing. When he handed in his paper he was covered in sweat. He went out of the examination hall and staggered towards the house grounds, walking alone, according to his new and strange ways.

By a coincidence, Sulola was in the Peugeot waiting for Bafemi. She had come to say farewell before leaving to take up a number of fresh contracts in Lagos. She believed that it was her last meeting with the boy, because of her firm decision to remove herself from Tunji's life and revert to her usual independent outlook. She was responding to her maternal instinct. Never had she so much realised the pain of childlessness until she met Bafemi. She waited in the car two hours before the examination finished.

She saw him approach. He was frail in the distance, walking unsteadily with a disturbing lightness of foot. She came out of the car still wondering if he was well. He saw her and she at once became a magnification of all the things that he resented. He stood still. He was swaying lifelessly on his feet. The bile of anger, the turmoil of emotion increased his dizziness. He staggered forward. Sulola ran towards him. He still struggled mentally, but his knees buckled under. He lurched forward.

When he passed out it was in Sulola's hands. Two other students who witnessed the fainting fit helped Sulola carry Bafemi into the car. A message was left for the principal. Before the car reached the school gate, the boy was mumbling: 'Woli. Woli . . . Woli . . . '

Sulola drove to the private doctor. Tunji was called. The boy still mentioned the name of Woli. Tunji did not know where Woli lived. All these years he had never bothered to find out where the Adept lived. Bayo was summoned.

'Doctor, let's take him to Woli,' Bayo persuaded the private doctor. The small company drove to the Adept's.

The Adept received his neophyte and admitted him into one of his chambers for a rehabilitation of mind and body. Sulola went back to her house and brought along the paintings she bought from Althea. They all stood round the boy as he regained his consciousness.

Eleven

It was the painting, propped up against the wall, that he saw first. His eyes roved along the wall. There was another painting. He discovered the four paintings. The boy sat up, as if it was a dream. Sulola told him how she bought them from Althea. It was her intention to persuade him to come home. It was her intention to prove her love by providing the money he needed and make sure he could again be re-united with his father.

Bafemi slowly asked why Sulola allowed him to go when he came for the paintings, in spite of the burglar alarm.

'I wanted you to be free. At that time it was no use holding you back. You needed a taste of the outside to appreciate the home. I felt no force should be used on you.'

Events moved faster the next few days. Mary was summoned again. Realising how empty his architectural wonder-house was, Tunji appealed for a reconciliation with Mary. His hopes of a marriage with Sulola had fallen flat with their entrance into the Adept's.

It had been said that there was no advertisement made to ensure an entry to the Adept's. Only those who needed the Grace went there. When Sulola passed through the chambers of those who were there for rehabilitation, and her eyes met the Iya Abiye's, all her sufferings instinctively came to an end. The woman, Sulola, who was said to be rendered sterile after the birth of two children, knelt before Iya Abiye, who assured her of future maternal joys.

Seyidi drove to the south, furiously attempting to win Mary back. He found the Adept's as he was meant to. The Adept saw him and welcomed him. A movement through the chambers showed the answer to that craving in the Doctor. It was his constant wish to know how to heal without the trappings of modern psychiatry.

The Adept and the Doctor held a conversation. It ended with Seyidi's deicision to stay to, as he put it, 'work and worship'.

Bafemi recovered under the radiance of the Grace. Tunji went to the north and made the traditional reparations to Mary's parents. Mary accepted, thinking to herself that unhappiness was merely an absence of the Grace. The past years rolled away into one yesterday.

Sulola went deeper into Iya Abiye's chambers, throwing her Lagos contracts overboard, determined to be washed clean as the insulting Ogbo Imule had once demanded. Her sophistication gave way to the simplicity that was reflected in the pure tones of whiteness in Iya Abiye's attire.

Bafemi recovered from the illness that the obsession of recent years had imposed on him. He revived his lessons of the Lord's Prayer. He caught glimpses of Sulola and at last understood her affection and her need for children. His heart softened towards her, appreciating for the first time her frank intentions in the past.

Bafemi had enough time to paint for a week, in secret, before he left the Adept's. He painted only one picture and kept it from everybody else as a pleasant surprise. At his father's instigation, a two-day exhibition of his works was to be held for him at school.

Jones incorporated it into a school social activity. The parents and staff were invited, as the first appreciation of the boy's immense contribution to the school's successes in the arts festivals.

The introduction and opening of the exhibition were performed by the art master. Althea stood beside a large portrait painted in oils. It represented Sulola. Her sharp and steady eyes looked through the colours with life.

The art master spoke of the trophies won by the boy right from the first form, his tireless efforts and singular talent.

Bafemi was amused by the art master's praise. His eyes went to where Althea stood. Sulola's painting stood there, strangely like an idol to be worshipped.

Tunji entered, accompanied by Mary. Yemi, his half-brother, trotted in. Ayodele was with them. She waved to her brother, giggling almost too loud. Bayo Cole felt happy for his apprentice, to whom the Adept always endeavoured to impart knowledge, making an adult of him. Mama entered, her face beaming with pride. Althea still stood by Sulola's image.

The exhibition was officially declared open. Bafemi moved across the hall. People moved round the works. He stood in a corner, watching the entrance. Sulola arrived, her new simplicity marked by a sympathetic blue dress.

Bafemi's eyes were on Sulola. Mary watched her son. Althea carried the painting to Sulola and said: 'It is yours.' Sulola stared unbelieving. For all she knew, this was more natural than a photograph. She knew that she had never posed for Bafemi. She looked up. Her eyes met Bafemi's. He was already walking towards her.

'Woman, each step of your gait deserves respect, for you have been the most frank of us all. Each beam of your smile deserves gratitude. Smile, woman. Smile at me. I have wronged you. Have we not all been vulgar? Gather me in your arms like a mother her son or a son his mother. To you I am most grateful.'

Bafemi's parents saw him.

Sulola regarded him, her eyes filling up like his. Bafemi stood in front of Sulola. Althea still held the painting. His gaze held on, in a line, like the eternal force of life. He uttered two words, his eyes on Sulola's with liquid fusion.

'Thank you.'

Seyidi was to know Sulola later at the Adept's. As if his fate had been linked with older women, he assisted Iya Abiye in the therapy for Sulola. The society woman gave away the lustre of sophistication, learning to know love and do away with lust. Seyidi helped her. Perhaps later, they would be one.

Odo-Ode remained as it was, because, according to Woli Daniel, the Grace was absent, for only the presence of the Grace made any home building a success. Bafemi and Althea came always as they grew in age, avidly learning what the Grace meant. They understood early how important it was to build a home before an establishment, appreciating with more depth that no self-reproach was necessary when they remembered that they had once made lust not love.

Farewell to Babylon

Bode Sowande

Three original plays by one of Nigeria's leading playwrights, well-known as the founder of Odu-Themes drama group in Ibadan.

The Night Before centres on a group of students reminiscing on the eve of their graduation. Their memories gather pace and reach a climax with an experience of disillusionment and betrayal.

Farewell to Babylon is to some extent a sequel to *The Night Before*. Two of the former student comrades meet again in an ironic encounter during a farmers' revolt, and the clash of their ambitions and allegiances leads to a tragic climax.

A Sanctus for Women is an adaption of a Yoruba folktale. Desperate for a solution to her destitute plight, a woman trader offers her daughter to the Iroko spirit.

Drumbeat 13
ISBN 0 582 64233 7

The Contract

Festus Iyayi

Wherever you go, whatever you do, the price has to be paid. Not just the usual price for service or supply, but the percentage on top. This is the story of one man who resolved to rise above the system, to resist all attempts to draw him into the same game. But the forces of corruption are too strong.

Like many another, Ogie Obala finds the road to hell paved with good intentions, and on the way he finds that love represents another form of corruption, of betrayal and of loss.

Festus Iyayu's second novel is a worthy successor to *Violence* (Drumbeat 1).

Drumbeat 34
ISBN 0 582 78524 3